DADDY ISSUES

MIA CLARK

Cherrylily

ISBN: 1974561771
ISBN-13: 978-1974561773

Book design by Cerys du Lys
Cover design by Cerys du Lys
Cover Image © Depositphotos | majdansky

Cherrylily.com

Erica, thank you for helping me come up with the idea for this book, whether you meant to or not. It's a fun story!

CONTENTS

Acknowledgements   vii

1. Introduction   1
2. Grey   3
3. Grey   7
4. Grey   11
5. Fiona   17
6. Fiona   21
7. Grey   27
8. Fiona   31
9. Grey   35
10. Fiona   39
11. Grey   43
12. Fiona   47
13. Grey   53
14. Fiona   59
15. Grey   69
16. Fiona   73
17. Grey   77
18. Fiona   81
19. Grey   85
20. Fiona   91
21. Grey   93
22. Fiona   99
23. Grey   107
24. Fiona   113
25. Grey   121
26. Fiona   131
27. Grey   137
28. Fiona   151
29. Grey   159
30. Fiona   163

31. Grey   171
32. Fiona   179

    A Note from Mia   183

STEPBROTHER WITH BENEFITS 1 (TEASER)

1. Introduction   189
2. Ashley   195
3. Ethan   199

    About the Author   205

ACKNOWLEDGEMENTS

Thanks for taking a chance on my book!

I really like taboo and forbidden romance, but I like to do it with a twist that makes it a little sweeter and fun instead of just steamy and sex-filled.

Now, don't get me wrong, I'm a fan of as much steami-ness as a story calls for, and some stories call for a lot more than others, but...

This isn't just a book about a girl who likes to call a guy "Daddy." I mean, Fiona does really like calling Grey that, but there's more to both of them and I hope you'll agree with me once everything's said and done.

I like the forbidden aspects, but to me it's just a gateway towards bringing two people together more intensely than they could ever come together without that.

Enjoy!

①
INTRODUCTION

Do you know how fucking difficult it is to concentrate when you have the ass of an eighteen year old girl wearing yoga pants in your face? Seriously, do you?

I didn't ask for this. I wanted to do yoga. Legitimate yoga. This isn't supposed to be some kind of set up for an x-rated movie. I'm not supposed to be staring at Fiona's fine as fuck curves, and I'm definitely not supposed to notice that her yoga pants are so tight that I can literally see every inch of her pussy in glorious detail through the thin, stretchy fabric.

I probably shouldn't add that this girl's camel toe is to die for.

And, hold up. Let's take a break for a second. What do you think's going to happen when I die from it? Obviously I'm going to hell. There's three very good reasons for that, too.

The first reason is that I'm twelve years older than her. The second is that she's my younger sister's best friend.

What about the third one? Are you really going to make me tell you? Fuck you. This is already hard enough as it is.

"Am I doing this right, *Daddy?*" Fiona asks, looking over her shoulder at me?

Yeah... I'm screwed.

2

GREY

Before you judge me, I want to explain how this all happened. It's not like I go around staring at girls that are younger than me. I don't go to yoga class just to check out hot eighteen year old girls, either. I'm not that kind of guy. Fiona's an exception, and there's one huge reason for that, but I need to tell you how it came to this.

My sister and I grew up with just each other. Emily, I mean. Fuck! Emily's my sister, and Fiona is Emily's friend. I'm not that fucking twisted. Holy shit, get your mind out of the gutter. I am *not* related to Fiona. I don't even fucking know why I have to explain this shit.

Anyways... my parents died when I was younger. Yeah, let that sink in for a second. I'm this eighteen year old kid and I'm sitting at home one night babysitting my six year old sister. Suddenly a cop comes to the door and I think it's some kind of prank or something. My friends liked to do that shit sometimes. Call the cops on each other saying the music was too loud or whatever. I wasn't playing music, and Emily was sleeping, so this is how that went:

I answer the front door wearing pajama pants and a t-shirt. This pair of cops is standing outside, looking serious as fuck. Like, I have no reason to be scared of the police, but whatever is going down right now needs my full attention.

"Grey?" one of the cops asks. "Are you Grey Royal?"

"Yes," I say, but I regret my decision instantly.

The cop next to him makes this sound that's kind of somewhere between pain and horror. It's like this whole ordeal physically hurts him and also he's terrified at what's coming next. I don't even know why, because I feel like I'm the one who should be terrified right now, but whatever.

"Can we come in?" the first officer asks. "Is your sister home? There's something we need to tell you, son."

I've always heard it's a bad idea to just let police come into your house. I have nothing to hide, though. I'm a pretty good kid, especially at eighteen. I'm not going to say I've never smoked pot or drank while underage, but I'm not hiding anything now and I don't make a habit of it. I have pretty good grades, I play on the football team in school, and...

Well, none of that matters right now.

The police come into the house and we go sit in the living room. I offer them the couch and I take the recliner next to it.

"Do you guys want something to drink?" I ask.

"Sure," the first says.

"Water?" the second asks. His throat sounds dry.

I go to get three glasses of water, because I think I need one for myself, too. It's a little hard bringing them all back to the living room, so it takes me awhile. On my way there, before I turn through the door, I hear them talking.

"Seriously, how are we supposed to tell this kid his parents are dead?" I think it's the second cop, because I don't recognize his voice. The only thing I've heard him say before now is "Water?"

"That's part of our job. To protect and to serve. It's not all glamorous, buddy. You have to deal with the hard problems that no one will ever thank you for along with the heroic ones that'll get your name in the news."

That's all great. I appreciate his work ethic. But...

My parents are dead?

I dropped those glasses of water, by the way. I stood in the doorway to my living room, staring blankly at nothing, and I dropped the glasses of water I was carrying. The police officers helped me clean everything up and then they sat me down and quietly explained everything.

3

GREY

I didn't tell Emily about our parents at first. How the fuck do you explain to your six year old sister that she's never going to see her parents again? I mean, I guess you just do it. You sit her down like the cops sat me down and you explain to her that a drunk driver crashed into our mom and dad's car when they were on their way back home. Smashed up everything, destroyed the car, ruined two people's lives.

The drunk driver died, too. I don't know if that's a blessing or a curse. Sometimes I kind of wish the guy was rotting in prison for the rest of his life, and sometimes I'm grateful that he's dead so I don't have the urge to murder someone.

I told Emily eventually. It didn't take that long. I told her a few days after it happened, when she was starting to get real skeptical about the fact that I kept insisting our parents went away on a vacation without telling her. Also, the fact that more of our relatives kept showing up at our house and acting sad and depressed didn't help.

"Yeah, so..." I say to her. "Uh... that vacation I told you about? The one mom and dad are on?"

"Uh huh?" she says, looking up quietly from her Barbie Dreamhouse.

Ken's just chilling outside while Barbie takes a nap and Stacie plays with the cat. The rest of Barbie's sisters are packed up in Emily's toy chest, though.

"The vacation is in heaven," I tell her. "They... they're not coming back, Emily."

"I know," she says softly. "I heard Auntie talking about it the other day."

"Wait, what? Why didn't you say anything?"

"You looked really sad, Grey. I didn't want you to be sadder."

So I'm over here worrying about how to tell my little sister that our parents are dead and she's worrying about me being sad? This is deep. I can't deal with this right now.

"I am sad," I tell her. "It's not because of you, though. I just..."

"I miss them, Grey, but I didn't want to cry in front of you because I didn't want to make you sad," Emily says.

"Hey, come here," I say, except we both kind of go to each other. "You can cry in front of me. I'm sorry. I was worried about crying in front of you, too, but... you can cry, Emily. It's alright. I'm still here, and I know mom and dad are gone and it's going to be rough, but... I'm still here, and I'm not going anywhere, and--"

She cuddles up against me and I'm not sure if she's crying or not at first, but she is. I'm crying, too. I don't know when that started. It just did. Don't ask. The next thing I know I'm laying on the floor, waking up. We both fell asleep. Emily's still sleeping, too. Ken's still outside the dreamhouse, and Barbie's taking a nap, and Stacie's still hanging out with the cat.

4

GREY

This is all real depressing, and I completely understand that. I'm older now. I'm not trying to make you cry over here. I'm just trying to explain to you how I became a father.

Wait, what? I know that's what you're asking yourself.

Yeah, sort of. I mean, I'm technically a big brother, but Emily was young, and over time she started calling me Daddy. I think it was easier for the both of us. You go to a parent-teacher conference for your younger sister, because you're her guardian now, and it's kind of like, what the fuck am I supposed to say?

Do I explain the whole drunk driver accidental death thing? I really don't want to bring that up again. So I just introduce myself as Emily's dad, and Emily starts calling me, Daddy, and I get that might sound kind of weird, but whatever. I'm doing my best over here.

When Emily started going to high school, she met this girl named Fiona. They became best friends pretty quick, too. Emily had a hard time making friends before that, but she made friends with Fiona in like... a day. They were always together after that. Fiona starts hanging out at our house all the time. It's cool. Whatever.

I wasn't supposed to hear it, but I overheard her talking to Emily about her mom once. Apparently it's kind of bad over there. Not all mom's are created equally, and not all dad's are the best, which is evident by the fact that Fiona's left her and her mom before she was born. Great guy, obviously.

And... instead of explaining my own kind of screwed up situation to Fiona's mom when Fiona wanted to sleep over or come over or do whatever, I ended up introducing myself as Emily's dad. Same thing as with the teachers. It's just easier, alright? Don't fucking judge me.

Fiona knew, though. Emily and her share everything. Literally everything, as you're about to witness.

"Can I call him Daddy, too?" Fiona asks Emily one day. They're just sitting in the living room, doing homework while listening to music.

"I don't know. I think so?" Emily says to her.

I'm sitting there doing work on my laptop, but nobody's asking me what I think, so I just keep at it.

Until Emily says, "Grey, can Fiona call you Daddy, too?"

"Uh, I guess so?" I say.

In my head I'm thinking this is just two teenage girls being weird and the fun is going to die down quick. If you just give in and accept it, they'll get bored faster, it won't be entertaining anymore, and they'll move on.

Right? I'm not crazy thinking that, am I? Pretty fucking sure that's how it works.

"Alright, *Daddy*," Fiona says, curling her tongue around the word.

Emily laughs like they're sharing a joke. Fiona giggles, too. It doesn't take long for them to go back to their homework, though. That's it then? I don't have to deal with this anymore?

Good. Real fucking good. Because I don't know if I can. There's something about the way Fiona said it, and the way she looked at me, and... with her lips quirked into this wicked grin while she looked up at me under her lashes and her voice took on this teasing, sexual tone.

Holy shit. I don't think my cock has ever twitched that hard before.

To be fair, I never had much of a chance to date while growing up. I had to take care of Emily, remember? Now that she could sort of take care of herself, I was trying to get back into the swing of it, but it's not like it's easy. You try going from having a high school girlfriend to a bunch of quickly failing relationships while attempting to go to college, run a new company what with your parents giving it to you in their will, taking care of a six year old for eight years until she's mostly able to take care of herself, and...

Let's add the fact that with Fiona over here all the time, she had a serious knack for popping up at the worst possible moment whenever I had a girl over. I swear this girl has a sixth sense. I'm sitting on the couch watching a movie with some girl I met last week, and things are progressing, or I think they're going to, and I'm about to go in for a kiss, and...

Fiona shows up. To be fair, Emily does, too. Sort of ruins the mood, you know? I can't exactly complain about being cockblocked by my sister and her friend, though.

Except then Fiona starts calling me Daddy, so...

New scenario for you:

I'm making dinner with another girl, and Fiona and Emily are out. This is going well. I'm making out with this girl while we're waiting for the timer on the oven to go off. We've got a few minutes. It's getting hot and heavy. I lift her onto the counter, she wraps her legs around me.

Suddenly she whispers, "By the way, Grey... I'm not wearing any panties..."

Which is basically my cue to unzip my pants, pull out my cock, and fuck her on the counter. Right? Which I'm doing! Or I'm trying to. This is going places.

And then Emily and Fiona come home early. Fuck. I zip my pants back up and slide the girl I'm with off the counter. She fixes her skirt, but looks pretty fucking annoyed. I get it. I feel the same.

"Hi, Daddy!" Emily says, skipping into the kitchen.

"We're home, *Daddy*," Fiona adds. I swear she just says this because I'm with a girl.

Also, my cock twitches right then, too. Fuck.

"Ummm..." the girl says, obviously confused. "You didn't tell me you had kids?"

"No, uh... this is my sister," I tell her. "My sister and her best friend. It's..."

It's complicated, which is why I didn't get into it yet. I

was going to, I swear, but can't I just have one night to myself?

If that's not the worst, you know what else is complicated? I had to raise Emily by myself for eight years, I had to deal with having almost no dating life, and then getting cockblocked by my sister and her best friend for another four years. And now, after all of that?

Emily's eighteen. She's an adult now, I guess. Something like that.

Fiona's eighteen, too. And she keeps hanging around my house, going swimming, wearing a bikini, wearing the skimpiest fucking pajamas I've ever seen. Legs for days, the poutiest fucking lips, eyes I could stare into forever if I didn't stop myself, curves in all the right places.

And she still calls me Daddy.

5

FIONA

"**A**lright, *Daddy*..."

It started out as a way to tease him. I know Grey is Emily's older brother, even if she always calls him Daddy. It doesn't mean anything to her except that he's always been there for her. He's like a father to her, and...

I've never had a father. I've never called anyone Daddy before. I think that's what the original appeal was for me. My mom always dated these new guys, usually a new one every couple of months. Sometimes they'd get cocky and tell me I could start calling them Dad if I want. They never stuck around, though. Also, they're gross old men and I seriously can't ever see what my mom sees in them.

So the day I asked Emily if I could start calling Grey "Daddy," too, um... I was doing it more to tease him than anything. Grey's nice, and he's sweet to Emily, and he's always been great to me. He lets me stay over whenever I want, which is nice because of that whole thing where my mom has another sleazeball over all the time every few months.

I guess the thing is that I never really understood what it was like to call someone Daddy before, so...

When I did it for the first time, it was like all of a sudden something strange happened to me. I didn't even mean to, but the first time I said it to him, I *felt* it, too. Do you know what that's like? When you call someone something and you immediately feel an intense emotional connection to them? That's the only way I can explain it.

I'm not saying I thought of Grey as my father, either. I still don't. Not really. It's just, um...

I *really* like calling him Daddy...

I only meant to do it a few times to tease him. A few times turned into doing it basically every time I saw him, though. For a month, then a year, and Emily and I have been best friends for over four years now, and I've known Grey for almost that long, too.

It probably helps that he's the exact mental picture of a daddy to me. And by that, I don't exactly mean I want him to be mine. Um... I mean...

I *do* want him to take care of me. I wish he could. I know that's not going to happen. He's Emily's older brother, and he's twelve years older than us. He has girls around the house sometimes and I try not to get jealous, but it's hard.

He's just a great daddy, you know? He's a good father figure, I mean. If I were going to have children, I'd want it to be with someone like Grey, because I'd want my babies to have a daddy like him and not like the father I have.

I don't even know my father's name. I think part of the reason is because my mom doesn't know his name, either. She refuses to admit it, though.

Grey, my fake daddy, is strong, he's sweet, he's always looked out for me. He doesn't treat me like I'm annoying or that he doesn't want me around. He spends time with me and Emily. He's got really sexy abs. We've gone swimming at the beach together, and I used to just wear a one-piece swimsuit, but I bought a bikini just to see if I could get Daddy to look at me. His jaw has that chiseled look that comes with age, and a stupidly handsome scruff of facial hair. Not a full beard, but he's not clean-shaven, either. It's just enough that you can feel a prick of it as it tickles your lips when you kiss his cheek.

Which, I do, because, you know, Emily does it sometimes, and I want to do it, too.

What's wrong with kissing Daddy's cheek?

The thing that's probably wrong is I'd like to kiss him all over, and I'd love if he kissed me everywhere, too. My cheeks, my lips, kissing a trail down my neck, cupping my breasts in his hand and kissing around them in circles until he reached my nipples and pulled them into his mouth... and lower... *oh my...*

Sorry, Daddy. I want to be your good girl, but sometimes you make it so hard.

Or I want to make you hard...

It's definitely one of those things. I think you know which.

6

FIONA

addy issues. With Grey, it's complicated. Let's just put those aside for a second, shall we? I'm on the phone with Emily right now, so I don't have time to get into it.

"I wish you were going to college with me, Fi," Emily whines. "I'm going to miss you too much."

"It's only an hour away," I tell her. "I'll come visit you all the time. Like, every weekend or maybe sometimes during the week. Stop calling me Fi, too. It reminds me of a dog's name."

"What, like Fifi?" Emily asks, trying to hide a giggle. "That's why I like it."

"*Emi*," I say, doing the same thing to her. "No. No Fifi-ing me! Don't even start! I'm not a dog."

"Oh, I don't know. I know a lot of guys call you a bitch, so..."

"That's because I won't sleep with them," I tell her. "That's not my fault, it's theirs."

"They aren't all *that* bad," she says. "Some were pretty cute. You could have at least gone on a date with one of them."

"I know I *could* have," I say. "I just don't want to."

Why would I want to go on a date with a high school boy when I could spend more time with Emily and Daddy instead? Not that I've ever told Emily that. I like spending time with her, too, but whenever I get to see Grey at the same time... *yesss...*

Which is about as far as my romantic relationships have ever gone: Unrequited. Oh well.

"When are you and Daddy driving to college?" I ask her. "Tomorrow, right?"

"Yup. In the morning," she says. "Do you want to come with us? Maybe we can find some cute guys at college and we can double date or something."

"I don't know if that's a good idea," I say. Mostly I'm talking about the double dating, but I don't know if I can go with her, either. "I'm trying to look for a job. It's not exactly the easiest. It's hard explaining to places that I'm fresh out of high school and not planning on going to college anytime soon. They don't believe me, or else they want someone with more experience and an education."

"I bet Daddy would hire you if you asked him," Emily says. "He's doing really well lately. Always says he needs a personal assistant now. He says it like he's joking, but I bet if you asked him he would hire you in an instant."

"Yeah... I don't know if that's a good idea, either," I mumble.

My mind flashes to thoughts of me and Daddy sitting

in his office at home, him with his pants off, and me hiding under his desk. Oh, the things I would do to him...

"Just think about it, alright? I think it would be fun. Then it'd be easier for you to get time off to come visit me, too. Or you could both come and you could be his assistant for the trip. Like a work trip, but you get to have fun at the same time. How great would that be?"

"I doubt that's how it works," I tell her, laughing. "I'll think about it, though. It really could be fun."

I don't think my idea of fun is the same as Emily's right now, but whatever.

"You should come over soon," Emily says. "Daddy and I are going to spend the day together before I head to college. I want to see you! I bet he does, too."

"Well, yeah, duh," I say with a grin. "I'm heading out the door now. I was just waiting for you to ask."

"Pft! You don't have to wait," she says. "You're always welcome here, Fi."

"Fiona!" I shout at her through the phone, laughing. "Come on, Emily, don't do this to me."

"Fine... Fiona..." she says, like I've ruined her entire world.

"Shut up," I tell her, grinning. "I'll be right over. See you soon."

We hang up, and I try to sneak out of my mom's tiny apartment without her noticing. Her man of the day decides to get up and go to the bathroom right then, though. He opens the door to my mom's bedroom and gives me the most disgusting, full body, up and down look before heading down the hall. My mom notices me standing there on my way to the front door.

"Fiona," she says, stopping me. "Where are you going?"

"I'm going to Emily's house," I tell her. "Her and her... her dad... they're doing some stuff before she goes away to college and they invited me."

"Oh," she says, giving me a look. "Well, don't get any ideas while you're there."

"Mom, I'm not getting any ideas."

"You know I can't afford to send you to college," she says, ignoring me.

"You can get student loans for it," I remind her. "Plenty of people do it."

"Yeah, they do, and then they wind up broke and without a job and all the money they make goes towards paying back what they owe, but it takes fifty years, and by the time they're done they've got nothing to show for it. I know, Fiona. I know."

I don't bother asking my mom how someone ends up without a job but then somehow all the money they make goes to their student loans. I also don't correct her and tell her that no student loan nowadays would be on a fifty year payment cycle. I've looked into this a lot, because even if she doesn't want me to do it, I'm an adult and I can make my own decisions.

Or, I can when I'm older. It's just harder now. In order to get financial aid, I sort of need my mom to help by filing a FAFSA form for me, and I think we both know how she feels about that. Once I'm twenty-four I can fill it out inde-pendently, though. It sucks, and I wish I could just go to college now, but maybe saving up for six years is a better idea. I don't know.

"I'll be home later," I tell my mom, refusing to get into this now. Nothing I say is going to change her mind. Believe me, I've tried.

My mom's *boyfriend du jour* comes out of the bathroom right about then. I catch him staring at my ass, and when I give him a dirty look because of it, he just winks at me like we're sharing some kind of secret. It's not a secret that you're a douchebag, Tony.

"See you later, baby girl," Tony says as he brushes past me while I hurry to leave.

"We should do something as a family soon, Fiona!" my mom shouts out to me before I open the door to head out into the real world. "You, me, and Tony!"

I ignore her and shut the door behind me. Tony's not family, Mom. I don't care what you think.

Anyways, I already have a Daddy.

7

GREY

I'm just minding my own business in the living room, doing work on my laptop, when my sister pops in and sits on my lap. I get it, and she's trying to be cute or something, but seriously, Emily? She just grabs my laptop out of my lap, puts it on the coffee table, and sits right the fuck down.

"Daddy, you know I love you, right?" she says.

Which is great and all. I love you, too, Emily. But...

"What do you want?" I ask her. "Money or something?"

She pouts at me, which I admit is pretty cute, but she's my sister and she should really use her pouting skills on someone else. Like, by going to get a boyfriend and asking him for money. Except then I'd have to deal with her having a boyfriend. Oh shit. I'm not prepared for that. I don't think I'll ever be ready for it.

"Why do you think I want money?" she asks, hands on her hips like I've offended her greatly. "I just wanted to tell you that Fifi is coming over soon."

"Who the hell is Fifi?" I ask her. "Wait, fuck. Is that what this is about? You bought a dog?"

"Fiona!" she says. "Actually, she said that, too. Told me to stop calling her Fi because it reminded me of a dog's name."

Now, I'm not proud of where my mind goes after hearing this. I just want you to know that. I'm not proud at all, but...

Fiona. Dog. Doggystyle? Fiona on my bed, her ass in the air, chest down, breasts pressed against my blankets, while I thrust hard into her from behind.

And obviously she calls me Daddy, because that's what Fiona does. Fuck.

Fuck me, Daddy...

She's not even fucking here yet, and she's already doing this to me? Holy shit.

"So she's hanging out with us for the day?" I ask, all casual, nonchalant, no fucks given. Play it cool, Grey.

"Yup! Is that alright?" Emily asks.

"You don't have to ask, Emily," I tell her. "Fiona comes over all the time. I don't care. I'll get her a key if you want."

Which I immediately realize is a terrible idea, because once Emily's gone away to college, if Fiona just starts popping in to hang out, and I have a girl around, uh... yeah, I can basically never have a girl around. Also I don't know how I would handle being around Fiona by myself. I'd like to think I am a strong man with infinite willpower, but...

"I know, right?" Emily says, distracting me. "You're like Fiona's daddy now, so it's cool. Thanks for looking out for both of us, Grey. You're the best older brother and daddy a girl could ask for."

"Uh, thanks," I say to her. "You're pretty cool, too."

"I know," she says, grinning at me. "That's why I said that before."

"Said what?" I ask, because I'm not even sure what she said, and also I'm trying hard to get images of Fiona and I going at it doggystyle out of my head.

"You know that I love you? That."

"Oh," I say, laughing. "Yeah, I know, Emily. I love you, too. You're great. Fiona's alright, too. I'll hang out with you guys whenever you want."

"Good," she says. "I know Fiona appreciates it, too. I'm going to miss you, Daddy."

FIONA

I get to Emily and Daddy's house. He's doing some work on his laptop, so Emily and I go upstairs to her room. She basically drags me there, but it's probably for the best. I don't know why, but ever since I turned eighteen, I've started thinking about... um...

I'm an adult now, right? A *woman*, even. Which means that Daddy and I could legally, um...

That's a big UMMMmmm.

Don't mind me, I'm just umm-ing to myself over here. I can't talk about this to Emily, so you're it. You're the one who has to listen to me.

"So, I had an idea," Emily says once we're in her room. She hops onto her bed, sitting crosslegged, and I join her.

"What's up?" I ask her. "What are we doing?"

"Let's plan a surprise for Daddy," she says.

Oh, I've got a few surprises I wouldn't mind planning for him, alright...

I don't say that, though. Because, you know, um...

"What kind of surprise?" I ask instead.

"Grey's been my daddy for... well, it's a long time now. I kind of feel bad, Fiona. I know he's really just my brother, but he's taken care of me so much and he didn't have to, you know? He took over our parents company after they died and built it up to where it is now, and I know he enjoys it, but it's something that I don't think he ever wanted to do. He did it because he had to and he wanted to take care of me, so I just want to do something in return for him."

"I get it," I say with a smile. Emily's always so cute when she gets like this. I like how her and Grey have a really strong bond.

"Sooo... what I was thinking is we should plan a fun weekend for him next week. I told him I'd probably be too busy at college to come back home on my first weekend at school, but that's just so he doesn't suspect anything. What do you think?"

"I think it's a cool idea, but how are you going to get back home?" I ask her.

"Bus or something," she says. "Or you can come pick me up maybe? If your mom lets you borrow the car?"

Yeah... about that... I give her a look and she basically understands without me saying a word.

"I bet Daddy would let you borrow his car if you asked?" Emily says. "You could tell him you've got a date and you wanted to drive yourself to be safe."

The thought of telling Daddy I have a date with someone else is... no. I already feel like dying. My cheeks are burning red just thinking about it. Actually doing it?

Um, no. Unless it's a date with *him*, but in that case, he could drive us. And that's not going to happen, so it doesn't even matter.

"Ooohhh!" Emily says, bouncing up and down on her bed. "Did I guess something? Am I close? Do you have a crush on a boy, Fiona?"

"What! No?" I say. "Ummm... no. Nope. That's not it. I was... I was just thinking of something else. Yup. That's it."

"What were you thinking about?" Emily asks, oblivious.

"Um, I don't know? I mean, I guess I was thinking about how Grey's great. He's been like a dad to me, too. I'm glad I met you both. I'm really glad we're friends, Emily. I wouldn't want anything to come between us, so it's hard that you're going away to college. I'll miss you."

"Aww, that's sweet," Emily says, smiling at me. "I'll miss you, too. Don't tell him I told you this, but Grey likes being your daddy, too. It's cute the way he talks about you sometimes."

Wait, he talks about me? Except I cant ask Emily about this. I don't even know how to start.

"Maybe we have daddy issues," I say with a nod. Then I realize what I just said and my cheeks burn even brighter than before.

"Maybe probably," Emily says with a laugh. "Not the same, though."

"But different," I say, agreeing with her. "Not the same at all."

I am one-hundred percent sure that my "Daddy Issues" are completely different from Emily's. Just saying. I don't know if Emily would understand. It's not like I'd expect her to, either. It'd basically ruin our relationship. Like, oh, by the way, I've had a huge crush on your brother for four years, and I know I call him Daddy just like you do, but I'd also really love it if he could take my virginity.

And, you know, *things*. What things? Don't ask. I may only be eighteen with no real experience to speak of, but I've got quite the imagination, let me tell you.

I've read plenty of romance novels to know exactly what I'd like to do with Daddy. I know what I want him to do to me, too.

Please, Daddy... I promise I'll be a good girl...

"Let's go tell Daddy to stop doing work and spend time with us," Emily says, slipping off the bed and to her feet.

"Is he busy, though?" I ask. "Maybe we shouldn't bother him."

"He's just screwing around. He already told me to come get him when we're ready. I mean, yeah, he's doing work, but he technically took the weekend off so we could hang out and then drive to my college after."

Screwing around. With Daddy. Definitely on my list of interests.

Apparently I'm not as much of a good girl as I'd like to believe. Sorry, Daddy.

9
GREY

I'm just sitting here, watching TV, minding my own business, when two eighteen year old girls plop down into my lap. One of them is my sister, so she barely counts. The other is Fiona, and I'm not even going to talk about that.

I was watching the news. The fucking news, guys! The way I feel right now, I might as well have been caught watching porn or something. I'm not even doing anything wrong. I'm just fucking sitting here. I was minding my own damn business! Fuck.

"Hi, Daddy!" they both say perfectly at the same time, as if they've practiced this. I wouldn't even put it past them, either.

"Hey," I say, trying to feign disinterest. Pretty fucking hard considering how close Fiona's ass is to my cock, though. "Are you two ready or what?"

"Yup," Emily says. "We are."

Fiona's about to say something, but then she almost

slips. I only have so much lap to go around, you know? I reach out and grab Fiona's hip, pulling her back and helping to keep her balanced. This is great and all, but then I realize I'm sitting here, my hand resting on Fiona's hip, while she sits in my lap.

Basically I get an instant erection, which is awkward as fuck considering my sister is on my other knee. I stand up quick and slide them off, then make some bullshit excuse so I can go into the kitchen. They follow me, though.

"Sooo..." Emily says. "What's the plan?"

"I thought we could go out to eat," I tell her. "Somewhere nice. Then we can come back here and watch a movie or play a game or whatever you want. Nothing crazy, just something nice."

"Oh," Emily says, with this weird look on her face.

"What's that supposed to mean?" I ask her.

"Well... I'd really love to go to Lucca's for Italian food," she says.

"Yeah, I figured, which is why I already made reservations," I tell her.

"But..."

"Uh, but what?" I ask, confused.

There shouldn't be any *buts* here, though. Lucca's is Emily's favorite restaurant. We've gone there for basically ten of her last twelve birthdays, and a bunch of other random ass special occasions, too. Emily got an A on her math test? Let's go to Lucca's!

"Emily's trying to watch her figure," Fiona chimes in. "It's this new diet she's doing."

"It's not a *diet*, Fiona," Emily says, rolling her eyes. "It's a *lifestyle*."

"Whatever it is, it's dumb," Fiona says. "It's just some pasta, Emily."

"Yeah, but I'm going away to school and I need to have good eating habits. I don't know what they're going to have in the college cafeteria. Or what if I have a lot of homework to do for my classes so I can't exercise as much? This is important."

"Listen, I already made the reservations, and it's just one meal before you go away," I say. "I think you can make an exception."

"It's not about that," Emily says. "Obviously we're going to go. It's just that I promised myself that if I wanted to eat something a little unhealthy then I'd exercise first. Which means we have to exercise before we go. Is that alright? Do we have time?"

I look at the microwave clock. It's barely afternoon, so...

"Yeah, we've got plenty of time. Reservations are for four. We have like... three hours. I think we're good. You go do your exercise or whatever and I'll watch TV."

"What? No, you have to exercise, too," Emily says, pouting at me.

Like I've said before, my sister pouting at me has no real effect. She's my sister.

"Yup!" Fiona says. "*Please, Daddy?*"

Fiona pouts, too. We're not going to talk about this. I'm not going to tell you that my erection was mostly under control after a minute or so in the kitchen, and now it's a completely raging hard-on again. Not even fucking talking about it. No fucking way.

"Fine," I say, because I need them to stop pouting immediately. Mostly Fiona, but if Emily's pouting, Fiona's going to keep it up, too. "What kind of exercise are we doing?"

"Yoga!" Emily says, clapping her hands together and jumping up and down like a little kid. She's my little sister, so I guess it works.

"Why did I let you convince me to get into yoga again?" I ask her.

"Because it's fun?" Emily says. "Duh."

"Because Emily has a crush on one of our instructors," Fiona adds.

"I do not!" Emily screeches at her. "I mean, he's cute, but... he's Daddy's age, so..."

Fiona's cheeks burn bright red. I don't know what that's about. I'm not even going to ask. I'm still trying to keep my throbbing cock under control. I think it's working. I can do this. Willpower.

"I don't think we have time to go to a yoga class right now," I say. "We completely missed the morning one, and the afternoon one isn't until later."

"We're going to have to improvise," Emily says with a devious look on her face.

"Mua ha ha!" Fiona cackles.

"You two aren't the villains in some sort of fucked up spy movie that somehow involves doing yoga," I remind them. "Cut it out."

10

FIONA

"**W**e can just do yoga here," Emily says. "I've been doing these yoga videos through DailyBurn sometimes and they're a little different than what we do in class, but it's the same sort of thing. If we move the coffee table and maybe the couch a little we should have plenty of room in the living room. It'll be fun."

Daddy thinks about it. He looks at Emily for most of this, but then he sneaks me a quick peek, too. I don't know what thoughts are hiding behind his eyes, but I'm sure they aren't the sort that I'd like him to be thinking.

I still think about it, though. I think about what it'd be like if he wanted me. I think about all of the interesting things we could do with the flexibility we've gained from taking yoga lessons.

I've gone to them with Emily and Grey since Emily managed to convince him a few years ago. The older girls in our classes always seem to flirt with him, too. It probably helps that he's basically the only guy who does it with us unless you count one of our instructors. The instructor only shows up half the time, though. The other half of the time it's a woman.

One time Daddy did end up going on a date with one of the girls from class. She was kind of pushy and snooty, though. I think that's the only reason he did it. I can kind of see why someone would want to date her. I'm sure plenty of guys are interested in a hot woman who does yoga, at least as far as a one night stand goes, but...

Daddy deserves better. Which is probably the reason I kind of maybe sort of sabotaged their date. I mean, I didn't come out and obviously ruin it, but I helped it go badly before he accidentally slept with her. It's not even really my fault, either. She's a bitch and I think Daddy just went on a date with her because he's been lonely and needed company.

And maybe some release. Sexual release, you know? I can help with that. I wouldn't mind, at least. Blue balls hurt, right? I don't want Daddy to be in pain...

"Alright, let's go change," Emily says to us. "Meet back in the living room in ten minutes?"

"What?" I ask. I'm slightly disoriented from daydreaming about Daddy's cock. Whoops.

"We're going to change into our yoga clothes," Emily says. "Come on, Fiona."

"Um, I don't have mine with me," I tell her. "I didn't know we were going to do yoga."

"It's cool," she says. "You can borrow some of mine. Don't worry about it."

Which sounds great in theory. I mean, I'm fine with it.

Except after I try on what she gives me I remember the reason Emily and I don't share clothes.

"Ummmm," I say, standing there in my borrowed yoga pants and tank top.

"It's fine," Emily says, raising one eyebrow and biting her bottom lip. "It's not like we're going out like this."

This is what Emily considers "fine," just so you know:

Emily's smaller than me. We look kind of similar in that our body types are basically the same, but she's a couple inches shorter and so everything else about her is a little bit smaller, too. We're both in shape, but in this case it really doesn't matter.

Her yoga pants fit me in the sense that they stretch and I'm wearing them, but that's about it. They're tight. Very tight. I can feel thin stretchy fabric riding up my butt and wedging itself between my thighs. I'm not even going to bother looking, but I know for a fact I have the biggest camel toe right now.

The tank top is slightly better, but my breasts are a little bigger than Emily's. So combine the fact that she's slightly smaller overall, and my breasts are slightly bigger, and you basically get a tank top that smashes my breasts together and makes me look like I'm really trying to put on a show.

"Are you really going to keep your bra on?" Emily asks, confused. "It's going to get all sweaty."

"Emily, your sports bras definitely won't fit me. I barely managed to get this tank top on as it is," I remind her.

"What about one of my bras?" she asks me. "It won't be as tight, so I think it'll work."

She fishes through her dresser for a regular bra and tosses it to me. I catch it and go to change again. It doesn't take too long, but...

"Well, like I said, it's not like we're going out like this," Emily says with a shrug. "It's not a big deal."

It might not be a big deal to her, but my boobs literally look huge right now. Her bra is too small for me, which just presses them together and pushes them up. Combine that with a tank top that's too tight and basically I'm pretty sure I now look like I have the biggest breasts in the world. And I'm wearing very tight yoga pants. I don't even know.

"It's just us," Emily reminds me. "Don't worry about it."

Us. Me and her.

And Daddy...

GREY

W hat the hell have I gotten myself into?

I change into my yoga clothes. It's basically just sweat pants and a t-shirt. They make yoga pants for guys, but they're nothing like the ones girls wear. They're... basically just sweat pants. I don't know what to tell you there.

Our living room is pretty open when it's cleared away, so before Emily and Fiona come back down I get to work pushing stuff aside. It's not like there's a ton to do on that front. I push back the two side recliners, one all the way against the wall and the other out into the open concept hallway off to the side. We have another kind of open concept door leading into the dining room behind the living room, so I slide the couch out there. That just leaves us with the coffee table and I'm not going to be able to lift that one on my own.

We can bring it out into the hallway and move it back after. That's the plan, and I'm over here waiting for Emily and Fiona to come back down to do it. Except when they come back down, I suddenly realize I've forgotten how to breathe.

Emily is fine. I know what she looks like in her yoga clothes. It's yoga pants with a tank top and a sports bra underneath. Pretty standard.

I've seen Fiona in her yoga outfit before. Admittedly, I try hard not to stare at Fiona in her yoga outfit. Thank God she changes in and out of it just for the yoga classes we go to. I only have to deal with it during our lessons, and she's usually over with Emily so I can make some excuse to go off to the other side of the room or whatever.

Which is great and all, but this isn't Fiona's usual yoga attire. Not even close.

"I told Fiona not to worry because it's just us," Emily says. "Right?"

"Uh, yeah..." I say. "Right..."

"Is this alright, Daddy?" Fiona asks me, fidgeting in place.

Please don't ask me that right now, Fiona. Just please don't. I'm glad I have a pair of boxer briefs on under my sweat pants or else I'd have the most obvious erection in the world right now. I can't even guarantee you it's not obvious already. Who the fuck knows? I'm not about to look down at my cock and draw attention to myself.

"Let's just, uh... let's move the coffee table into the hall-way," I say, trying to distract myself. "Then we should have plenty of room in here for all of us."

"It might be a tight fit, but I know we can do it!" Emily says, cheery.

You know what else is definitely a tight fit? My cock in Fiona's pussy. You know how I know this? I can see every fucking intricate detail of her pussy right now.

Letting her use Emily's yoga pants was probably not the best idea. The only saving grace I have right now, and the reason I can sort of convince myself I'm not going to hell, is that I wasn't the one to suggest it. Emily did it. This is all her fault.

I go to one side of the coffee table and bend slightly to lift it up. Emily and Fiona take the other side between the two of them. This is great, and we're lifting the thing and carrying it into the hallway, but more problems keep popping up.

Mostly, Fiona has to keep her hands pretty close together to grab her side of the coffee table. A side effect of this is that if her breasts weren't already almost popping out of her bra and tank top they definitely are now. Her arms press her breasts together even more, as if they weren't already looking massive to begin with.

Fiona's usual breasts are fine. They don't need to look massive. They're a little more than a handful, and I appreciate that.

I'm a guy, though. Sometimes we just want to stare at huge breasts, I guess. I don't know how the fuck this works. It's just a thing. Needless to say, as much as I try, I literally can't pull my eyes away from Fiona's bouncing, gloriously amazing, huge as fuck breasts popping out right in front of me.

I really tried for a few seconds, too. I tried and I failed. I don't know what else to tell you.

We set the coffee table down into the hall and I quickly turn around. I need to calm the fuck down. Somehow my erection is erect. Like, it was erect, and now it's more erect. I didn't know this was possible, but it just happened.

"I'll set up the DailyBurn yoga stuff," Emily says, skipping past me and into the living room.

She does some stuff with our TV and soon enough we're good to go. Sort of. It's nowhere near as easy as that.

FIONA

Well, *hello there*, Daddy. I don't know what I've done to deserve this, but it looks like you have a present for me? I'd really like to give you something, too...

...Is not what I say, but I think it! I think it a lot.

At first I'm embarrassed to let Daddy see me this way. I know Emily says it's just us, but I've never acted obviously slutty in front of him. I mean, sometimes Emily and I talk during sleepovers or whatever, and we can definitely um... do the talking part of that whole "talk the talk" thing, but neither of us has done any walking. We do not walk the walk.

So the fact that I'm standing in front of Daddy in a yoga outfit that's too tight and looks kind of slutty on me is embarrassing at first, but then when I see Daddy's reaction. *Oh my*...

I don't think Emily notices. She's kind of blind to that sort of thing. Not that I'm the most knowledgeable and experienced girl, either. If Daddy weren't wearing sweat pants that clearly show a juicy outline of his cock I would probably just think he had something in his pocket. Maybe his wallet or cell phone or I don't know.

It makes me wonder if I've missed seeing his beautiful erect cock before now? I hope not. I've always wondered, and I don't think that makes me a good girl, but for Daddy I would try to be very *very* good...

"Are we ready?" Emily asks, hopping away from the TV and taking up her starting yoga position.

"Yeah," Grey says, grunting the word.

"Ready!" I say, clapping once.

I feel kind of slutty again, because the only reason I clapped was so I could push my arms together a little and make my boobs bounce. I want to see if Daddy will notice and what he'll do if he does.

I don't have a chance to figure it out, though. The yoga lesson starts and we get right into it.

We begin with simple poses while we're standing up. Mountain, and then Warrior, with a few variations here and there. We realize we have a problem after we finish our first set of Warrior poses. Emily pauses the routine with the TV remote.

"I guess the living room is kind of a tight fit," Emily says, contemplative.

"Yeah..." Daddy says. "I can go hang out in my room while you two finish up if you want."

"No no no," Emily says, shaking her head. "Here, let's do this."

We were all in a line before, Daddy in the middle with Emily and myself on either side of him. Emily scoots her brother back a little, and moves me away slightly, then she goes to the side next to both of us, sort of in between. Now we're more like a triangle than a line, and it does give us a little more room to work with.

"I think this'll work," Emily says. Before me or Daddy can object, she continues our TV yoga lessons.

We do a Tree pose, then Triangle. So far so good, and we do have a lot more room to work with like this. Eventually we head to the floor for some ground poses, though. And, um...

I'm sorry, Daddy?

The lesson picks up a little from here. We go into a Upward Facing Dog pose, which shifts into a Cow, immediately to Cat, and ending with Downward Facing Dog. It's kind of a fast transition, but they're all things I've done before so it's not too complicated. The first time I do it, I almost tip over at the last transition, though.

"Careful!" Emily says, smiling over at me.

Daddy doesn't say anything, and it's at that exact moment when I realize what sort of view he has. It's my butt. And my thighs. Might as well add everything in between my thighs, because these yoga pants aren't hiding anything.

I look over and give Emily an encouraging smile, but in reality I'm trying to see if I can sneak a peek at Daddy. I'm happy to report that I can.

The next time we do our Dog-Cow-Cat-Dog transition, I pretend to slip a little. I don't know why. I'm being bad right now. Daddy might have to punish me later. I know he won't, but it's so tempting, and I don't know if I'll ever have this chance again.

I look over my shoulder at Grey and I smile.

"Am I doing this right, *Daddy?*" I ask him. "How's my form?"

It's really cute how hard Daddy's trying not to stare at my ass. He pulls his gaze away from my butt and looks me in the eyes, doing his best to smile back at me.

"Uh... good," he says, swallowing hard. "You're doing good, Fiona. Just do the transition slowly and it's not that hard. Take your time."

"Alright, Daddy. Thank you."

I go slower next time. I tease it out, moving as slow as I can while still following along with the instructor on the TV. Emily performs her yoga poses next to us, completely oblivious. When we shift into our Cat-Cow poses, I pretend that I'm getting ready for Daddy's cock. He's waiting and about to thrust into me. When we go into Upward Facing Dog, I imagine that Daddy's cock is deep inside me and I'm laying on his bed, my back arched up while ecstasy pounds into me over and over.

I want it so bad...

We do more yoga, and each and every pose suddenly feels sexual to me. I don't think this is what meditation and zen is like. Maybe tantric meditation. I wonder if Daddy would do some tantric yoga with me? The kind where our bodies come together in different positions and it's almost like we're having sex. I'm sure we could have sex at the same time, which would make it even more fun, don't you think?

The instructor finishes with a soothing "Namaste" and a gentle bow. I'm breathing heavy at this point. That was definitely a workout, but not the kind I expected. Emily's sweaty, too. Daddy is...

...hurrying out of the living room and heading to his bedroom down the hall.

"Grey?" Emily calls after him. "Are you alright?"

"Yeah," he says. "Just hot. I'm going to take a shower. You two clean up and then let's head to dinner."

"Um... sure..." Emily says, confused. To me, she adds, "Do you think that was too hard for him? I know it's different for guys, but I don't think that was any worse than our usual yoga class."

I shrug. "There were some parts that might have been a little harder," I say.

And by that I mean I'm pretty sure Daddy's cock was harder. I hope Emily didn't notice me teasing him. As much as I enjoyed that, um...

Emily's my best friend and I really don't want to ruin anything between us. He's hers, too, and I realize that. I know it's in a different way, but even still, that's what makes this harder for me. I can't, and yet I want to, and...

"Do you mind if I take a shower first?" Emily asks me. "I'll try not to be too long. I'll bet you can use Daddy's shower if he finishes before me. I'll let you borrow my makeup after, too."

"Sure," I say, smiling.

Emily gives me a quick hug and then runs up the stairs to her room. Daddy's bedroom is on the first floor down the hall.

I keep smiling and I try not to smirk, but, um...

I'm going to be good. I won't be bad. I can't be bad. I need to be a good girl for Daddy, which means I definitely can't do what I want to do.

Except I really want to do it...

GREY

I can't even. Literally can't. I'm done. I am completely fucking finished and I don't know what the fuck just happened, but I can't do it. No. Stop, Grey. Don't even fucking start.

She's twelve years younger than you, and she's your sister's best friend, and the girl calls you Daddy for fuck's sake. That should mean something. Like, oh, I don't know, stop thinking about fucking the shit out of her?

Kind of hard considering her ass was just in my face for half an hour. I'm pretty sure I could draw an accurate and extremely detailed picture of her pussy right about now, too. Except I can't draw, so we're going to skip that one. I can remember it in detail, though. Yoga pants or not, that shit is forever going to be seared into my memory from now on.

Which is real fucking bad. My erection went from bad to worse, a full hard-on, no chance of hiding it. So I ran down the hall to get in the shower before Emily noticed. Fiona, too. Except I barely even fucking care with Fiona anymore. I'm tempted to drag her ass out of her shower, throw her onto my bed, and ravage the fuck out of her.

I can't even fucking believe this. What kind of person am I? Fuck.

I don't think this erection is going away, though. That's kind of a problem considering we're all supposed to go out to dinner. How am I going to explain that one? I can only shift around so much before it becomes obvious.

I can just imagine it now:

"Why are you moving around so much, Daddy?" Emily asks me.

"Yeah, what's wrong, *Daddy?*" Fiona adds, smirking.

"Oh, don't mind me, girls. I've just got a raging hard-on remembering Fiona's pussy in my face earlier. Just a normal day in 'I'm Really Fucked Up'-ville."

We're not having that conversation. I'm not even going to entertain the possibility of having anything remotely close to that conversation. Which means only one thing. I know what I have to do.

As soon as I get to my room I shut the door and head to my private bathroom. This used to be our parents room. It took me a few years to shift things around, but I thought it might be easier if I moved in here. Emily has the whole second floor to herself, and I took the first floor. We don't have to share a bathroom and we can each have our privacy.

That was kind of the idea, at least. I don't know if it

worked out like that. Emily spends more time downstairs with me than upstairs. My office is upstairs now, too. Almost every time I'm downstairs, she comes down. When I go up, she "coincidentally" goes up. Sometimes I worry about what's going to happen when she goes away to college.

Even that isn't working. My cock is *still* hard, and I *still* can't get the image of Fiona's perfect fucking curves out of my head. I might have a problem. I definitely have an erection, but I don't know if that's a problem or not. Is it still considered bad if you have an erection for four hours even if you haven't taken Viagra? It hasn't even been an hour for me yet, but I think I could hold onto this one for four or five easy.

This ties into that whole "I know what I have to do" thing I mentioned earlier. I'm getting to it. Just fucking hold on.

I strip down fast, toss my clothes onto my bed, and go into my bathroom. I turn the shower on, make sure everything's nice and steamy and warm, and then I step in. I don't immediately start taking a shower, though. Nah, that's too simple.

I wrap my fingers around my cock. I stroke myself fast at first, kind of wanting to get this over with. If I cum, I think I should be able to get rid of my erection for a few hours at least. I can make it through dinner and then I'll worry about the rest after that.

What's the rush, though? Emily and Fiona have to take a shower, and then they're going to want to do their makeup, and we still have a little more than an hour before we have to be at Lucca's for our reservations, so...

I slow down, teasing myself away from a hasty climax. It's not even that fucking quick, though. I've had an erection for the past thirty minutes and I don't think I can take anymore.

Just a *little* slower. A little bit, and...

I close my eyes and imagine Fiona without clothes on. It's not exactly hard. Like I said before, those yoga pants she borrowed from my sister didn't leave much to the imagination. I picture Fiona on my bed, her ass up, pussy wet with arousal. I kneel behind her, slowly moving forward, my cock bouncing in anticipation. In a few more seconds the head of my cock will be right between pussy lips, and a few seconds after that I'll feel her clenching hard onto my shaft while she whimpers and begs me to go slow.

"Please, Daddy... you're... you're so big... be gentle with me..."

Holy shit. Calm the fuck down, Grey.

I have to take my hand off my cock because I'm about to cum again. I'm barely even fucking doing anything and here I am ready to have the orgasm of a lifetime. What are you doing to me, Fiona?

This rhetorical question becomes a little too real in a few seconds.

I know I'm not holding my cock anymore, but suddenly *someone's* fingers are wrapped around my shaft. They're dainty and smaller than mine, and the nails are definitely longer. The hand moves slowly at first, kind of uncertain, like its never done this before. I'm refusing to accept that this hand belongs to anyone, and I think I can keep believing this if I just keep my eyes closed.

Yeah... even I'm not buying that one.

I open my eyes and look a little behind me to the side. Fiona's standing there, completely naked. My cock looks massive in her tiny hand. Her fingers don't even fit all the way around it.

"Fiona," I say with a grunt. I grab her wrist and stop her from slowly jerking me off. "What are you doing? You need to stop. We can't do this."

"Why not, *Daddy?*" she asks, trying to be all coy and seductive.

It almost sounds convincing, and I'm seriously about to explode right now, but...

I can tell by the look in her eyes and the slight tremor in her voice that she's nervous. It hurts. It hurts to stop her, because I feel like I'm about to have a serious case of blue balls, but it also hurts to see her this way. I don't want to hurt Fiona. I want to take care of her, to protect her. She's been through a lot of shit, and I know what that's like. I don't think I'm a hero or anything, but if I can help her then I really want to try.

I don't want to take advantage of her. Yeah, it's real fucking obvious at this point that she's got a crush on me, and I'm glad she waited until she was of a legal age to act on it, but, uh...

No. This really can't happen. It needs to stop. Now.

I don't know why I do what I do next. Probably because Fiona still thinks of me as *Daddy*, and sometimes Daddy's have to punish bad girls so they stop acting naughty.

That sounds a lot dirtier after I spell it out like that. Fuck. I blame my cock.

14

FIONA

Daddy grabs my wrist hard and carefully, but forcefully, peels my fingers away from his shaft. To be honest, I'm disappointed but... I'm also kind of relieved? I don't know why I thought this was a good idea. I just did. I knew Daddy had an erection after we finished up with yoga. Not only was that the simplest explanation for why he left so quick, but I caught a really tantalizing and exciting glimpse of the bulge of his cock thrusting against the front of his sweat pants.

I don't think Emily noticed. Emily also didn't notice me sneaking away to Daddy's room downstairs while she takes a shower. I should have, oh... *I don't know*... at least fifteen or twenty minutes with Daddy before I need to make my escape so Emily doesn't suspect anything?

That was the plan, at least. I'm not going to say it was a great plan or anything. At first I just wanted to sneak in and see if I could take a peek at Daddy's cock while he took a shower. I didn't know what he'd be doing in there, I swear! I mean, I had my suspicious, but...

Who knows? He could have decided to take a cold shower, you know? His erection might have been gone by the time I got here, and also maybe he could have locked the door to his bathroom, or else the glass door of the shower could have been all fogged up and I would only see a faint glimpse of the outline of Daddy's hard cock.

I just wanted to see it...

As soon as I saw it, I wanted more, though. I watched Daddy stroke himself. He pulled hard on his cock at first, but then he grunted and slowed down. Oh my God. Is that because of me, Daddy? Did you really get that excited from seeing me in Emily's too-tight yoga pants? Do you like staring at my ass, Daddy? Could you see my pussy pushed up tight against the stretchy fabric? Did you notice I was wet thinking about you staring at me, Daddy?

And, um... one bad idea leads to another, which basically means I sort of decided it was a good idea to strip down and play with myself in Daddy's bathroom. He didn't see me, though! Not yet. When he started stroking himself slower, I played with my clit. I moved as fast as he did, pretending he was rubbing the head of his cock against my slick folds, up and down, and then teasing my clit. I leaned against the wall and pushed two fingers tight inside me, imagining what it would feel like if that was Daddy's cock.

Daddy's cock looks like it's a lot bigger than just two of my fingers, though...

You're so big, Daddy. I want you inside me. Be gentle at

first, alright? I want to take all of you, Daddy, but I've never done this before, and... I'm so wet right now, Daddy. I'm so wet for you...

I nearly came right then and there, but then Daddy stopped stroking himself. Why? I don't want Daddy to stop. I hear it hurts if you stop. Will Daddy's balls really turn blue? That sounds painful, so...

I sneak into the shower with Daddy. We're both completely naked. The sound of the water falling all around us hides the fact that I'm there, so Daddy barely even realizes it when I gently wrap my fingers around his cock. His cock throbs and pulses in my hand. It feels so amazing. This is the first cock I've ever touched, the first one I've ever held tight in my fingers. I want it inside me, but right now this is for Daddy. This is just for you, Daddy...

Except, you know, it's not. He stops me. He grabs my wrist hard, forcefully peels my fingers away from his shaft. I think we've gone over this before. I just wanted you to know why I did what I did. I don't know if that makes it any better.

The both of us are still soaking wet from the shower. Daddy's more wet than I am, but I'm plenty wet right now. Um, I didn't mean it like that! That way's true too, though. Daddy drags me by my wrist to his bed and then he pushes me onto it. I bounce on the bed on my stomach, legs splayed, ass up towards Daddy. He grabs my ankles and pulls me back, bending me over the bed. My feet touch the ground right by his, but my upper body stays firmly on the bed, my breasts pressing hard against Daddy's covers.

"Fiona, I'm extremely disappointed in you," Daddy says, his voice throaty and harsh.

I know it shouldn't, but the way he's talking to me right now turns me on even more.

"I'm sorry, Daddy," I whimper, wriggling against the bed.

I don't mean to do that, either, but my clit keeps rubbing hard on his blankets and I just feel so sensitive right now. I've masturbated before, but I've never felt anything like what's happening right now. Is this what sex is like? But Daddy's not even inside me yet, so...

Is he *going* to be? I press my cheek against Daddy's bed and look behind me a little, trying to be covert. He looks down at me with anger in his eyes, which... I'm extremely wet right now and this isn't helping my cause. I'm really sorry, Daddy! I can't help it. I just...

I look down, trying to avoid his angry stare, but I think this is worse. I see Daddy's cock bobbing up and down mere inches away from the back of my thighs. Every few seconds he twitches and his cock starts bobbing fast for a little while, slowing down, and then... *twitch*.

"Is this how you were brought up?" he asks me. "I know you've had a hard time growing up with your mother, but I'd like to think that I taught you a little better than that. Do you see Emily going around and throwing herself at boys? No. You don't. You've been a very bad girl, Fiona."

I squirm. I really do want to be Daddy's good girl, but

for some reason I find it hot when he calls me his bad girl. This is so hard. I want him inside me so bad right now, but that would make me even naughtier, wouldn't it? Except if I'm Daddy's good girl I'll never be able to have him, will I?

"I didn't mean to, Daddy," I say to him. "I wouldn't! I don't want to be with other boys. I... I just want to be with you, Daddy. That's--"

While I try to explain myself to him, he interrupts me with a slap on my ass. His hand smacks hard against my butt and the sound echoes through the room. He's spanking me? Um, yes, he's spanking me! Holy hell.

I didn't know I'd like being spanked so much...

Daddy spanks my ass again and again. The right cheek, then the left cheek. It's not too hard, but it's definitely hard enough to feel something. The next time his palm slaps against my right cheek, I feel a rough sting, and then when he smacks my left cheek the sting spreads. I writhe beneath his heavy-handed palm, trying to move away a little while still accepting my punishment, but this just makes things worse. The blankets beneath me rub roughly against my clit, which makes me squirm even more, and the more I move, the more Daddy spanks me.

Until he doesn't. He stops and stares at me for a second. I don't know what he's doing because my face is buried in his blankets out of embarrassment. My cheeks are red. Probably both cheeks. All four. My face is burning, but so is my butt, and Daddy's just standing back there staring at me.

He lays his hand on the curves of my ass, no longer spanking me. His fingers tease lower until he gets to the back of my thigh. In, grabbing me, his fingers wrap around my leg, his palm tight against my sensitive inner thigh.

"Fiona," he says, his voice a rough mix of emotion. "Are you *enjoying* this?"

He doesn't ask me nicely. He sounds angry again. I shake my head fast. My nose tickles against the blankets and I accidentally let out a sneeze. I stop, embarrassed, and press my face hard into Daddy's bed.

"No, Daddy," I say, my voice muffled by his blankets. "I'm sorry."

"Don't lie to me," he says, squeezing my thigh tight.

He drags his hand higher until his index finger is pressed right against my arousal-slick slit. His thumb rests lightly on my butt, pressing inwards between my cheeks.

"Why are you wet, Fiona?" Daddy asks. "Do you think this is funny? Is this some kind of game to you?"

"No!" I say, pleading with him. "I don't think it's funny. It's not a game, Daddy. I... I'm just... I don't know... I can't help it. I'm sorry, Daddy. I'm really really sorry..."

"Do you understand the kind of message this sends?" Daddy asks me. "This is what I meant, Fiona. This is why I'm worried. This is why--"

He stops speaking with his words and talks with his fingers instead. He slides one finger rough against my clit, sending spasms through my body. Pressing it up and between my folds, he toys with me for a few seconds. That's all I expect, except then he pushes his finger deep inside me.

I can't. Oh my God, I can't. I can't handle this, I can't think, I can't...

I just can't. I can't even.

My body bucks up as soon as his finger is deep inside me. Daddy smacks his free hand hard against my ass and pushes me back down against his bed, though. He glides his finger in and out of me, pressing against spots inside me that I didn't even know existed.

I... Daddy, I... I'm your good girl, I promise, but I think I'm about to be very *very* bad if you don't...

He sends me over the edge with two fingers. My body trembles, an orgasm ripping through me. Why am I having an orgasm less than ten seconds after Daddy puts two fingers inside me? Why am I wetter than I've ever been after Daddy spanked me for being a bad girl? Why did I even think it was a good idea to spy on Daddy in the first place? Just to see his cock?

Um, obviously I'm a bad girl. I know it, and Daddy knows it, and I want to be his good girl, but I just keep doing bad things.

"I'm sorry, Daddy!" I whimper, my body betraying me. My voice betrays me, too, and my whimper turns into an ecstasy-induced scream.

Daddy doesn't say anything. He keeps fingering me with one hand while his other pushes hard against my ass, pinning me to the bed. My orgasm crashes through me, deep and hard. I ride it out until I can think a little better. Once my pussy stops clenching against Daddy's fingers, he slows down and gently slides them out of me.

"Do you understand now, Fiona?" he asks me.

I start to nod and say something, but then I look back. Daddy still has one palm pressed hard against my butt, holding me against the bed, but his other hand is holding his cock now. He strokes himself. Very very slowly. It's mesmerizing and I can't look away from his cock. I don't know how he's looking at me right now because the only thing I can see is the pulsing and twitching and throbbing of his shaft as he strokes himself slower and slower.

"Daddy," I say, but I don't know why I say it. "Please, Daddy... you can... please please *please*, Daddy, I want you to..."

"Fiona," he says, grunting. "Be quiet."

I barely have a chance to be quiet when I feel Daddy splashing against my back. I watch as jet after jet of his cum bursts from his cock. His sticky white cream lands between my shoulders at first, then more on the center of my back, another on my lower back, and finally a few more splashes land right on my ass. His cum drips down the curves of my butt, slipping between my cheeks, and I feel a little tiny bit tickling against my lower lips and joining the wetness of my own orgasm.

I lay on Daddy's bed, spent, covered in his seed. Not quite from head to toe, but close enough.

"Thank you, Daddy," I say, but I don't know why I say that.

"This... we shouldn't have done this," he says. "Fiona, I'm sorry. We can't do this. I didn't... I was just trying to punish you. I don't want you to get hurt. You can't just go into the shower with someone. That's not... I..."

Daddy stammers for words. The expression on his face is conflicted, and suddenly my heart aches for him.

"Are you going to be a good girl from now on?" he asks me, trying to stay calm, to keep his voice steady and strong. "Are you going to stop being naughty?"

"I'm sorry," I say to him. "I'll try, but... I don't know if I can stop thinking about your cock now, Daddy."

I'm just being honest! I'm not trying to start trouble. I'm not trying to be naughty. I don't want to be a bad girl...

"Fiona, you have to stop that," Daddy says, harsh. "We can't do this. You're Emily's friend. You don't know what you're saying. You don't understand."

I snap. I snap because he's wrong. I do know! I know exactly how I feel about him and I don't know why he doesn't understand that. I mean, I'm sorry for being a bad girl, but it doesn't change anything. It doesn't change how I feel, or what I want, or...

"I know what I'm saying!" I shriek at him. "I know exactly what I'm saying and I know what I want. It's not my fault you can't handle that, Grey!"

He steps back as if I've slapped him. I'm tempted to do just that, too! I don't, though. I'm too angry to even look at him. I'm too ashamed by what just happened and how it made me feel. I'm embarrassed to admit that I loved every second of it and I was hoping beyond hope that afterwards Grey would forgive me and we could finish showering together, and get dressed, and then cuddle in his bed.

And I didn't expect us to tell Emily right away. I know that's harder. I haven't even told her I have the biggest crush on Daddy, on her older brother, on...

I know it's going to be hard, but I want it so much, and to be told that I don't? That everything I feel is wrong?

I pick myself up off of Grey's bed and stomp away, storming into his bathroom. I slam the door hard behind me. And I lock it! I don't care! I'm taking a shower by myself!

"Fiona, I'm sorry," Daddy says, speaking softly through the door.

"Don't talk to me, Grey!" I shout back at him. Just in case he tries again, I turn the shower on to block out the sound of his voice.

"Don't even try to talk to me..." I whisper to myself. I know he can't hear me, but I don't care. I'm mad right now.

15

GREY

W ell, that ended really fucking badly. And how the fuck did you think it was going to end, Grey? Seriously, in what fucking world could that have ended well considering everything you just did to her?

Like, I get the punishment angle, alright? Maybe I shouldn't have done it, but Fiona was acting completely out of line, and... fuck if I know. I think she deserved to be punished is all I'm saying.

Is that why I spanked her? Or is it because I had a serious craving to press my palm hard against her ass, to feel her curves for myself after she sat there and fucking teased me for over thirty minutes while we did yoga with Emily? And then she just comes waltzing right the fuck into my private bathroom, strips down, and grabs my cock?

Holy shit was that hot. I have no fucking clue how I managed not to cum once she wrapped her fingers tight around my shaft and started jerking me off. I was pretty fucking close to begin with, but with Fiona's hand? Yeah...

Which is beside the point. Who gives a fuck if it felt good? This isn't about that. This is about Fiona realizing that she needs to be careful. Do you know what would have happened if she did that to any other guy? She could have gotten hurt. I like to think I'm a pretty nice person, but seeing her wiggling her ass in the air while she laid on her stomach on my bed, uh... yeah... I don't know how I managed not to straddle her like a wild fucking animal, shove my cock between her slick, plump pussy lips, and drive home the fact that I was hard as fuck over and over again.

I refrained. I controlled myself. Do you think boys Fiona's age could do that? No. And you know what? That's how you wind up pregnant, Fiona.

Shit. What if Fiona's pregnant? What if I...?

Yeah, I get that, generally speaking, you need to cum inside a girl to get her pregnant. I know how it works. I'm not a fucking idiot. It's just that it's the *cum* part that does it, and not necessarily your cock being inside a girl when you cum.

It's still kind of sinking in that after I spanked Fiona's ass red, after I noticed her inner thighs were seriously drenched because of how aroused she was, and when I plunged two fingers hard inside her... I don't know why I did that. I mean, I know *why* I did that, but I don't know why I did it.

In some insane part of my mind, I thought she'd realize that she shouldn't go waving her ass around at every guy in the world if I... fingered her. Listen, I'm not saying it makes sense right *now*, but at the time I thought it did. Lots of shit makes sense when you have an erection as thick as a fucking soda can and almost twice as long.

I didn't expect her to have an orgasm ten seconds after I thrust two fingers inside her. I had no fucking idea it'd be so easy to find her g-spot and make her cum. It was just there. It was right fucking there, front and center, and as soon as I touched it, I wanted to touch it more. As soon as she started spasming on my bed, I wanted to make her feel so fucking good.

Yes, Fiona was a bad girl. There's no way around it. You can't just go sneaking into Daddy's bathroom and start teasing him like that. You can't stroke Daddy's cock. You shouldn't be doing that with anyone, Fiona. Wait a little. Find someone you love, and who loves you, and...

We're not going to talk about this right now. We're not even going to think about it. Shut the fuck up. Leave me alone.

Making her cum was an accident. Ten seconds? I'm not going to say I set a world record today, but... yeah, I wouldn't be surprised. Just saying.

What happened after, though? I don't know. Why did I jerk myself off? I wasn't even going fast. Do you think that matters? No. No, it doesn't.

The point is, I came all over her back, my little baby-makers splashing between her shoulders, the center of her back, lower back, finally on her ass, and...

...sliding down her butt, between her cheeks, and most definitely onto her fine as fuck pussy lips. Do you think *none* of it managed to slip inside her? None. Absolutely no cum?

That's how you wind up pregnant, Fiona. That's exactly how you wind up pregnant.

Oh, don't worry, baby, I won't cum inside you.

I'm sure you've heard it before. It doesn't matter. How much sperm do you think it takes to make a baby? Let's just play a guessing game and figure this out.

Uh... one? It only takes one. Granted, the little fucker has to be lucky if he's literally the only one making a mad dash for BabyTown, but it's not like you need more than one. That's all it takes, folks. Just one.

Shit.

You know the worst part about all this? It's not even the fact that I did something monumentally stupid. It's not the fact that it's technically possible I just knocked up Fiona. It's unlikely, and I get that, but that's not even the worst of it.

The worst thing? It's the fact that after all of this it bothers me that she called me *Grey* instead of Daddy. Seriously, that's my name. Why should this bother me? It shouldn't. It kind of annoyed me when she started calling me Daddy, but then she just kept it up, and here we are today. Grey? When the fuck has she ever called me that? Emily does it sometimes, but not Fiona.

Why does this bother me so much? Why does it... hurt?

I have no idea. It's weird. I'm fucked up.

FIONA

'm angry! I'm very very incredibly frustratingly amazingly absurdly angry at Daddy. Who does he think he is? Yes, he's older than me. No, I don't have a lot of experience here. I mean, that was my *first* experience, so...

Except you know what? It doesn't count. Take that, Daddy! It's not even sex if you don't shove your tasty cock inside my slippery pussy, so... it's just not. I'm still a virgin. And maybe I won't let my first time be with you? What do you think of *that*, Daddy?

Wait! I'm sorry. I didn't mean that. I didn't mean to be naughty. I promise, I'm a good girl. I wouldn't do that. I learned my lesson, Daddy. I did, I...

I know Grey's mad at me, but I still want him to be my Daddy. I'm just... I *am* angry, and I don't like that he said those things to me, but...

I shower and try to calm down. I need to clean off

anyways. I'm sweaty from doing yoga with Daddy and Emily, but I'm also sweaty from what Daddy just did to me, and I've got Daddy's cum on my back and on my butt. That was really hot, actually. I wish Daddy had cum inside me instead, but I don't even know if that would work. Where would it all go? Daddy's cock is big and he came so much, and... I mean... I *want* it inside me, but I'm shorter and smaller than him, and I just don't know if it'll work.

Which makes me sad, actually. What if Daddy and I can never be together because my pussy is too small for his cock?

I frown in the shower while I clean myself off. I really hope that's not the case. I hope it isn't true. I just don't know, and I don't know if I'll ever know, because I need to be good and I can't be naughty, because it makes Daddy upset. I just...

Actually, you know what? Don't get me wrong, I'm still kind of angry. I'm starting to understand a little bit, but I don't appreciate Daddy treating me the way he did. I'm not talking about the spanking or cumming on me. I liked that. I mean the other part at the end with everything he said to me.

But, even if I'm still angry about that, um... well, *hello there!*

I'm washing myself, you know, as you do. I think most people wash themselves the same way, so I'm not going to get into the details. Anyways, I'm washing myself, and when I brush my fingers between my thighs to clean down there, um... *whoa.*

Like I just said, *hello there!*

I'm not masturbating or anything, it's just that everything feels different now. My pussy feels puffier? Daddy did that, didn't he? With his fingers. *Mhm.* I slide my fingers between my puffy pussy lips and feel how slick and slippery I am. Daddy did that, too. He did that to me.

Thank you, Daddy...

I think I understand a little better now. This is dangerous. I'm not even turned on, but I'm kind of turned on? I feel really good right now. My body feels nice even if it's just me cleaning myself off. I wish Daddy were cleaning me off, but maybe we shouldn't do that right now. Not right now, but...

Later? I mean, not immediately later. *Later* later. Like, sometime in the future. If I'm good. I'll be a good girl for you, Daddy. Promise!

But I can see what Daddy meant. What if I did this with another boy? Yes, I don't think he'd be as good as Daddy, but I can't say for certain that it wouldn't feel good. What if I did it with another boy my own age, and I thought of Daddy, so I kind of got caught up in the moment, and I imagined Daddy doing all of those things to me, but it's really just this other boy, and I don't like him, but I still have an orgasm, and then I feel bad and gross, but for whatever reason my body keeps responding afterwards, and I get all tingly and...

That's a mouthful.

Like Daddy's cock. Daddy's cock is actually probably more than a mouthful, at least for me.

The point being, Daddy's right and I need to be careful. I'm not going to admit this to him, though. I'm still angry at him. Maybe we can talk later about it. Maybe I'll ask him about a job like Emily mentioned to me earlier, and then Daddy will see what a good girl I can be, and instead of punishing me he'll reward me?

Hmmm...

GREY

Emily doesn't know. Thank God, Emily has no fucking clue.

Fiona finishes her shower and has the decency to come out wrapped in a towel instead of flaunting her body in front of me. I don't know if I'm happy about that one or if I'm disappointed. Maybe a mix of both. You already saw her naked, Grey. Calm the fuck down. This girl is eighteen and she's your little sister's best friend, so you really shouldn't be gawking at her to begin with.

I'm only thirty. I'm not dead. Fiona is drop-dead gorgeous right now, all shiny and wet, her skin glistening from the shower. That's not the same, though. That's nowhere near the same.

Holy shit, cut it out.

"Hmph!" Fiona humphs at me as she whisks past me, her clothes in her hands.

Oh, yeah. She left those in my bathroom. Uh...

And then, without a word, she opens my bedroom

door and steps out into the hall. I have no idea what the fuck she's thinking with that one. I'm just going to ignore it. If Emily comes crashing into my room and demanding shit from me, I'll deal with it then.

Like, oh, I don't know...

―――――――――――――――――――――――――――――

"Why did you spank my friend and then cum all over her ass, Grey? What the heck!"

―――――――――――――――――――――――――――――

Like I said, I don't know! Thankfully it doesn't fucking happen. Fiona doesn't come back, Emily doesn't show up, and I'm free to take a shower in peace this time. Mostly in peace. I still can't get the thought of Fiona's hot little pussy out of my head.

Two fingers. She was so fucking tight with just two of my fingers. Can I get my cock inside her? I don't know. I really have no fucking idea. I'm kind of leaning towards... no. Not that I don't want to try, it's just...

Wait. Fuck. No, I *don't* want to try! We just fucking talked about this! Dammit, Fiona!

I shower. I put clothes on. And I get the fuck out of my room.

At least I don't have an erection anymore. I'm not completely soft either, though. I'm a little hard, but I'll deal with it. I don't know what the fuck else you think I can do right now.

"Daddy!" Emily says, jumping to give me a hug when I meet her and Fiona in the living room.

"Hey," I say with a smile, hugging her back.

I have to force it at first, but I really am excited to take Emily out to dinner on her last night here before I drive her to college tomorrow.

"What took you so long?" she asks. "You took longer than me and Fiona combined."

"Uhhhh..." Fuck. What do I say?

"It was really nice of you to let Fiona use your shower after you were finished, though," Emily adds.

"Yeah," I say, because I have no idea what else to say. "Of course."

"Yup," Fiona says, smiling sweetly at me. "Thank you, *Daddy*."

Oh, fuck. You know that partial hard-on I was talking about a little while ago?

Yeah, uh...

Fucking, Fiona...

I didn't mean it like that. Fuck you. You know exactly what I meant!

"Are you two ready?" I say, pulling my phone out of my pocket and checking the time. "We've only got about thirty minutes before our reservation at Lucca's."

"Yay!" Emily says, clapping her hands.

"This'll be so nice," Fiona says to her. "What kind of movie do you want to watch after? Should we rent one when we're out or find something on Netflix when we come back?"

"Hmmmm..." Emily says, tapping her chin. "That's a good question."

"Why don't you two get your asses in the car and think about it on the drive to Lucca's," I say with a grunt.

"Alright, sorry, Daddy!" Emily says, giving me a quick apologetic hug. Then she runs to the front door, racing for the car.

"I'm sorry, too, *Daddy*..." Fiona says.

She also gives me a hug, pressing her breasts tight against my chest. And then she heads for the front door, but she kind of sashays her ass all the way there, hips swaying side to side.

You have no fucking clue how much I want to spank that ass right now.

18

FIONA

"**R**ight this way, ladies and gentleman," the host at Lucca's says to us. "The manager told me this reservation was for a special occasion so we've saved the best table in the house just for you."

Which personally I think is great, except Daddy seems less than amused once the man shows us to our seat. The host guides us through the regular dining area to a more private section near the back. There's still people sitting here, but everything looks a little different. Each table has a candle in the center of it and the lights above us are dimmed to create a cozy and romantic feel.

Yes, romantic. Which is probably why Daddy is less than amused right now. The host lays our menus on the table and waits for us to sit. We have a corner booth way in the back, set slightly away from the rest of the tables to offer a more intimate experience. It even has a curtain around it to give us the illusion of even more privacy. I mean, you can see through the curtain since it's more for decoration than anything, but still.

"Uh, here?" Daddy asks. "This booth?"

"Yes sir!" the host says. "It's our best. Everyone loves it."

"Who usually sits here?" Daddy asks.

"I'm not sure what you mean," the host says, confused.

"I mean, what kinds of people usually sit here? It's couples, isn't it? This looks like a pretty romantic table, so I think I can guess, but I want to hear you say it."

"Well, it certainly does offer a hint of the romantic," the host admits. "It's Italy, though. What do you expect?"

Daddy looks at the man, dumbfounded. Emily starts to giggle and I laugh, too.

"It's alright, Daddy," Emily says. "We can have a nice romantic dinner together!"

"Yeah, no offense, but--" Daddy starts to say.

Emily gives him her best puppy dog eyes, though. I join in, teasing him. I think we're teasing him for different reasons, though.

"*Please, Daddy?*" I say, batting my eyelashes at him.

"I think it'll be fun!" Emily adds. "We've never had a seat like this before. You should treat me good, Grey. I'm going away to college and who knows when you'll see me again."

Daddy grumbles and sits down in the booth with us. He's on the opposite side and slides all the way in. I don't know if he realizes it, but we're right across from each other now. Hmmm...

The host leaves us and a waitress comes by soon after to get us drinks.

"What can I start you with?" she asks, looking at us ladies first.

"What do you think, Fiona?" Emily asks me, nodding towards the menu.

"I think the answer is obvious, Emily," I say to her. "It *is* your last day and all."

"True, true..." Emily says, pretending to mull over her options.

Daddy looks at us with more than a hint of suspicion.

"Alright," Emily says. "I think we'll have a bottle of this *Tenuta San Guido Sassicaia* for the table."

"A wonderful choice!," the waitress says. "Can I just see your--"

"Yeah, no," Grey says. "No wine. They aren't even twenty-one, and even if they were, I'm not buying a three hundred dollar bottle of wine for these two. Water. Get them water."

"What!" Emily whines. "I wanted an Italian soda!"

Grey glares at her until she starts pouting at him, and then he caves a little. "Order it then, brat," he says.

"We have a nice--" the waitress starts to say.

"Red raspberry, please," Emily says.

"Can I get cherry cream?" I add.

"Of course, ladies," the woman says with a smile. "For you, sir?"

"I'll have a glass of that *Tenuta San Guido Sassicaia*," Grey says, smirking at me and Emily.

"A... a wonderful choice..." the waitress says, confused. "Can I just see your--"

Grey already has it out. He hands her his ID and she checks it quick before nodding politely to him.

"Anything else to start with?" she asks.

"I think we're good for now," he says.

"Bread!" Emily shouts out.

I don't know why she shouts, but it makes me laugh. Grey rolls his eyes at us and the waitress smiles but I think she's already tired of us. I don't know why. You can't blame us for trying to get wine, can you?

"I'll be right back with your drinks," she says. "If you need anything else, don't hesitate to ask."

GREY

Having visited Lucca's Italian restaurant many times over the years, there are a few things I've come to expect. The first is the porcelain statue of a fat chef they keep on every table. He sits there and guards the salt and pepper shakers like a pro. The next is good food. Not just good food, but pasta that's made fresh every day. I'm pretty impressed with that one. I tried making pasta with Emily once, and it wasn't exactly the hardest thing in the world, but I have no idea how anyone could make enough fresh pasta for an entire restaurant full of people.

The third and final thing I've come to expect from Lucca's is the music. It's kind of cheesy and cliché, but it's familiar and nice. I feel like I'm at home when I'm here. It's like family, and sometimes I worry Emily and I are lacking in those regards. I mean, we have family, but...

I don't know. You know what I mean?

We have Fiona, too, and I guess she's kind of like family. Speaking of Fiona...

One thing I don't expect when I come to Lucca's Italian restaurant is having my little sister's best friend try to play footsy with me under the table while my sister sits there, oblivious, eating her ravioli. I thought we had an understanding, Fiona? Why are you doing this to me?

I glare at her to try and get her to stop, but she just smiles sweetly at me like she's some kind of angel or something. Emily looks up from her food and glances over at me, at which point I kind of have to stop glaring at Fiona.

"Are you alright, Daddy?" Emily asks me. "You aren't eating?"

"Maybe he's distracted," Fiona says, winking at me quick before Emily notices.

"Oh, are you?" Emily asks.

"No," I say, gruff. I ignore Fiona's foot playing with mine and stab a piece of my chicken florentine, then shove it in my mouth. "I'm fine."

"Oh no..." Emily says, shaking her head.

Fiona's shoe is off now. She teases her toes up and under my pants, making skin to skin contact. I'm really fucking tempted to just kick her foot away, but with Emily right there, I'm not sure I can get away with it without her asking questions.

And then what do I say? Yeah, don't worry about it, Emily. Fiona's just playing footsies with me. No big deal. It's probably because I spanked her earlier and got her off. I thought we had a talk about this, but...

Yeah. Not doing it. You couldn't pay me enough.

"You like someone, don't you?" Emily asks me. "Who is it?"

Even Fiona blushes at that one. She stops playing with my foot and my leg, too.

"Uh, what?" I ask. "I have no clue what you're talking about."

"Is it a girl from work?" Emily asks.

"Emily, I don't have a crush on a girl at work," I tell her.

"Is it the waitress?"

"No, it's not the waitress."

"Is it... one of your clients? Is it a neighbor? Did you meet her in the grocery store? Have you gone on a date with her yet? When are you going to ask her out?"

"No. There's no girl. I don't like anyone. I have absolutely no interest in anyone whatsoever."

"Oh," Emily says, pausing to think. Then she starts to grin and laugh before she says anything else. Eventually she manages to spit it out, giggling uncontrollably the whole time. "Is it... Fiona?"

Fuck.

Uh...

Fiona's face radiates heat. Seriously, she might as well be the sun right now. I can feel it from here, and I'm pretty sure I could get a tan from her face alone. She swirls pasta around on her plate, but instead of taking a bite, she just keeps swirling and swirling it. Emily's over here cracking up, acting like she just told the funniest joke in the world.

I'm eating chicken. I can't do this.

"Sorry!" Emily says. "I was just teasing you two. Did you know Fiona has a crush on someone, Daddy? She won't tell me who, though. She won't admit it, either. I don't know why. Isn't that silly? I mean, like... really now...

if you have a crush on someone, you should probably just tell them. Maybe it's good to do something instead of telling them, though. Just go up and kiss them, you know? What do you think?"

"If Fiona has a crush on someone, I don't think she should just go up and kiss them," I say. "You don't know what kind of guy they are. He might get the wrong idea. That's how you get pregnant."

"Um, you don't get pregnant from kissing someone?" Emily says. "Even I know that."

"Yeah, well, what if he thinks the kiss means he has a free pass into your pants?" I ask.

"I guess..." Emily says with a shrug. "If Fiona likes him he's probably nice, though. She doesn't date anyone, so if she's got a crush, I bet she knows him better than that."

"That's what you think," I say, trying to steer this conversation somewhere else. "You never know, though. People keep secrets, Emily. It's not good to rush... into... anything..."

That last part? Where I stumble on my words? Yeah, that's because Fiona's foot is massaging my crotch. She went back to playing footsy with me, and I thought I had a great idea by ignoring her, but, no, I didn't. It wasn't a good idea at all, because what the fuck am I supposed to do now?

"I mean, you have a good point," Emily says, while her friend's toes curl around the outline of my shaft through my pants. "Maybe Fiona should invite him to the house sometime so you can meet him then?"

"Maybe Fiona should stop--" I start to say out loud without realizing it.

Yeah, I almost just told my sister maybe Fiona should stop feeling up my cock with her foot. Seriously, this is hard, and I'm hard, and this is hard. Everything's fucking hard today. It's difficult and it's hard, and I'm pissed off about all of it.

"You can't just stop liking someone," Emily says, confident and matter-of-fact. "It doesn't work like that."

"No, it doesn't," Fiona agrees with a nod. "But it doesn't matter, because Emily's wrong. I thought I liked someone, but I found out he's an asshole."

"Whoa, Fifi!" Emily says, laughing. "That's harsh. Who is it?"

"He's probably not an asshole," I say. "He probably just realizes that things could never work between you two for a lot of reasons. Just because you like someone doesn't mean you can be with them."

"Well... no!" Fiona says. "That's not true."

"It's definitely true."

"Are you two alright?" Emily asks. "Is this because you're hungry? I get kind of angry when I'm hungry, too. Just eat some food and it'll be fine. I'm halfway done my plate and it looks like both of you have barely started."

Yeah, well, you know what? I cut off a few more pieces of my chicken florentine and shove them in my mouth. Fiona glides her toes up and down my shaft a few more times before pulling her foot away. She twirls pasta onto her fork, plops it in her mouth, and chews defiantly.

"I'm going to the bathroom," Fiona says once she's done chewing.

She's got plenty more on her plate, so if Emily's hunger-anger theory is correct, Fiona's still plenty angry because she's barely eaten anything.

"Do you want me to come with you?" Emily asks.

"What's with girls and going to the bathroom together?" I ask them.

Emily makes a face at me like it should be obvious. Neither of them answers me, though. Emily slides out of our romantic table booth and lets Fiona out. And then, *stomp stomp stomp*, Fiona stomps away towards the bathroom in her strappy fucking sandals.

Seriously, you have no fucking clue how much I *still* want to spank that ass right now.

20

FIONA

D o you think it's true that Daddy and I can never be together? I... I mean... deep down in the bottom of my heart I know I've always wanted it, but wanting something doesn't mean it's going to happen.

For example, I want my mom to stop dating scummy guys. I want her to realize that she's worth more than she gives herself credit for, and I want her to have drive and passion in life. I've wanted these things for awhile, and I've tried to convince her, but she never listens to me.

So maybe...

This is stupid, and I hate myself the moment I start thinking it, but what if Daddy dates my mom instead? Then he would *actually* be my daddy. I mean, he's still my daddy no matter what, but he'd be my actual, honest to God, stepfather. And he's a good man, I know it. He would be good to her and he would treat her right.

Except I don't want that. Even thinking about Daddy with someone else makes my blood boil. I don't want to share him! I can't and I won't, and... but I can't have him to myself, either. Daddy's made this abundantly clear. He said it earlier, and even though I tried to tease and play with him during dinner he said basically the exact same thing just now.

"He probably just realizes that things could never work between you two for a lot of reasons. Just because you like someone doesn't mean you can be with them."

Well, that's great, Daddy, but it doesn't stop me from crushing on you hard, now does it?

I don't even need to go to the bathroom. I'm standing here, staring in the mirror, pretending to do my makeup. I don't even know why I'm doing that, because this is just one of those single person lady's rooms. I'm alone and no one else is going to come in, because I shut the door and...

...locked it...

Or not? Um... *hello there...*

GREY

"I'll be right back," I tell Emily a couple minutes after Fiona leaves the table.

"What? Where are you going?" she asks me.

"The bathroom," I say, which isn't exactly a lie. Maybe it's not the entire truth, either.

"Can I have a sip of your wine?"

"No," I say.

"Why not?" she asks, petulant. "You know, in Italy, basically everyone drinks wine. Even little kids. I mean, they probably don't have a lot, but it's completely normal! I'm just asking for a sip, Daddy. Please?"

"Yeah, not going to happen," I tell her. "If you want wine so bad, go to Italy. Don't even try it. In fact..."

Just in case she gets any bright ideas while I'm gone, I take my wine glass and finish off what's left. It's not like there's a lot, so don't think I'm going around chugging expensive wine. She sticks her tongue out at me and makes a face when I stand up to leave.

This should be the end of it, but when I'm halfway across the dining hall I turn around and see her soaking a piece of bread in my wine glass, sopping up the infinitesimal amount of wine that's left. Seriously, Emily, it's like four drops of wine. When she sees me glaring at her, she snatches the wine-soaked bread from my glass and plops it in her mouth, defiant.

Whatever. I don't have time for this right now. I'm going to go deal with someone far brattier than my little sister.

That's another reason I needed that last mouthful of wine. This is probably a terrible idea but I'm going ahead with it anyways.

I act like I'm heading to the men's room, which isn't much different from going to the women's room. They're both down a hall off to the side of the main dining area of Lucca's, and neither is a shared restroom like a lot of public ones. It's just one person per room, which works perfectly, because what I'm about to do requires privacy.

Also, it's easy, because Fiona left the door unlocked. Seriously, Fiona? You need to be more careful. This is even more of a reason for me to do what I'm about to do.

I open the door and slide my way in. As I suspected, she's not even using the bathroom. Fiona stands there, sulking, looking in the mirror. She almost looks like she's pretending to do her makeup, but she's got nothing in her hands to fix it up. And I know she left her handbag at the table with Emily, so...

When I close the door behind me, she notices me in the mirror. Startled, she jumps and opens her mouth to scream. Oh, no, don't do that, baby. Don't worry, it's just me. I put my hand over her mouth to stop her from screaming, but I kind of have to pull her back with me at the same time. She falls back into my arms and my chest. I reach behind us and lock the bathroom door.

"Shhh," I whisper into her ear.

She nods and stays still. I almost don't let her go, though. Fiona feels so good in my arms. She nuzzles back against me, getting comfortable, and I have a sudden urge to just wrap my arms around her and hold her tight like that.

That's for good girls, though. And as we all know, Fiona's been very very bad again.

I help her stand on her own. She looks at me through the mirror and frowns, but doesn't put up a fight.

"Fiona," I say, my voice a low growl.

"Yes, Daddy?" she asks, obedient.

"What were you doing back at the table during dinner?" I ask her. "Can you explain that to me?"

"Ummmm..." she murmurs, biting her bottom lip. "Teasing you, Daddy?"

"Fiona," I say again, a louder growl than before. "What *kind* of girl teases her daddy like that?"

"A bad girl, Daddy," she says, pouting at me. Not in a cute sort of pouty way, either. She's got a definite sad pout going on. "A naughty one. I'm sorry for teasing you, Daddy."

"I thought you learned your lesson before," I tell her. "Remember when you came in the shower when Daddy was trying to clean up after yoga?"

"Uh huh," she says, biting her lip again.

Holy shit, I have the strangest fucking erection right now. What the fuck is wrong with me?

"And you were a bad girl again, right?" I ask her. "What do you think that means, Fiona?"

"Daddy's going to punish me..." she says.

She doesn't just pout this time, she overdoes it. It's like the most exaggerated pout in the history of pouts, and yet it's also one of the most erotic things I've ever seen. Holy fucking shit, this girl is going to be the death of me.

"Put your hands on the sink, baby," I tell her. "Be a good girl for Daddy..."

Look, I know what you're thinking. Or maybe I don't. I have no fucking clue what I'm thinking. Daddy? Yeah, it's different. Emily is different. Fiona is different. With Emily it's one thing, and...

...with Fiona it's something completely different. I don't know how to explain it. You're just going to have to trust me on this one.

"Daddy?" Fiona asks, looking over her shoulder at me after she places her hands on the sink for me.

"Yes, baby?" I ask her.

"You've never called me that before," she muses. "*Baby...*" She tastes the word, letting it slowly roll off her tongue.

"Is that alright?" I ask her.

"I like it," she says. "Because I'm Daddy's, right? Daddy's girl. I'm trying to be Daddy's good girl, but sometimes I'm naughty so I'm Daddy's bad girl, and no matter what I'm Daddy's baby girl, so... is that right, Daddy?"

I freeze, because I'm not sure how to answer that. What was I just saying at dinner? We can't be together. I know this, which makes this more than a little complicated. What the fuck am I doing here? I should be ignoring her. I should just go back to the table with my sister, wait there, eat my fucking food, and go to bed early. Lock my fucking bedroom door so Fiona doesn't get any bright ideas and try to sneak in while I'm sleeping, too.

That's what I should do, but instead, I press my palm against her hip, slide it down to the hem of her sundress, and pull it up so I can spank her ass.

"Fiona, you *are* Daddy's girl, but... I... I don't know what that means. I don't think we can be together. I know what I'm saying and what I'm doing are confusing, and I don't even fucking know myself. I just... you should find someone your own age, baby."

"Daddy?" Fiona asks, looking back and smiling at me.

"What is it, baby?" I ask her.

"I'm ready for my spanking now," she says. "I know I've been naughty and I'm sorry, Daddy. I know you love me so that's why you have to punish me. It's alright, Daddy. I understand. Even if... even if we can't be together. I... I know, Daddy..."

FIONA

Smack.

Smack smack.

Smack, smack, smack.

Daddy spanks me again and again, but he's slower this time and gentler. My butt's still a little sore from earlier, but it doesn't hurt too much. I was naughty, and so Daddy has to punish me. It's not too bad. I kind of really like it, and I like that Daddy called me "baby" and I want to be Daddy's girl, no matter what that means.

I'll be your good girl, Daddy. Promise...

"Fiona?" Daddy says.

He hasn't spanked me for a little while, but I can feel his hand resting lightly on my butt. It's warm to the touch, and I'm not sure if it's because Daddy's palm is warm or if my butt is warm because he was spanking me.

"Yes, Daddy?" I ask him, being a good girl and looking straight ahead until he tells me he's done punishing me.

"Can you explain something for me?" he asks.

"What is it, Daddy?" I ask him.

"Baby, can you explain why you weren't wearing any underwear? What happened to your panties?"

Um... well... that's a good story...

"I... I didn't put any on to come to the restaurant," I tell him, honest.

"So you decided it was a good idea to go out wearing a cute summer dress that barely covers half your thighs and those strappy fucking sandals of yours, but no panties? Do you really think that's a good idea?"

"Ummmm..." I mumble. "No, probably not..."

"I think you're right," he says. "It's definitely not a good idea."

"I wore this dress and these heels for you, though," I tell him. "I know you like how my sandals have little heels and all the straps, Daddy. Remember how we bought them together and you said I looked very mature in them? And... don't you like the flowers on my dress, Daddy? You were there when I tried it on in the store, remember? You went shopping alone with me at the beginning of summer because I was embarrassed and my mom said she wouldn't help me get new clothes since I was eighteen already, but I didn't have a job yet. I didn't want to tell Emily, so you went with me and you helped me..."

It's silly, but I feel tears well up in the corner of my eyes. I know Grey isn't really my daddy, but he's always been there for me. He's more of a father to me than my actual father has ever been, especially considering I don't even know who that is. Grey's my daddy when my mom acts like she regrets having me half the time. I don't think she hates me, but I think she's glad I'm finally eighteen so I can move out on my own and she can try and forget the past eighteen years of her life.

Daddy comes close to me. He leaves one hand resting on my butt, but the other slides up and caresses my chin. He traces his fingers up my cheek to the tears that are threatening to come crashing down out of the corner of my eye. He wipes one away and kisses me softly on the neck.

"Why are you crying, Fiona?" he asks me. "We're all done, baby. That's it, alright. You're my good girl, right? You're Daddy's girl?"

"Uh huh, I know," I whisper to him. "You've always been there for me, Daddy. Grey. I... I'm not crying because of that. I'm crying because I love you. Not like... I mean... I don't know. Not like that. Maybe like that. I know you said we can't be together, Daddy. I understand that. Please don't leave me, though. I need you..."

"I'm here, baby," he says, kissing my neck, then my cheek, and then one soft kiss on the corner of my lips. "I love you too, Fiona. Not... I don't know. I don't know how I love you. Let's not worry about that right now, alright?"

"Alright," I say softly, nuzzling against his hand. He caresses my cheek softly, being so sweet and nice to me.

Daddy pushes closer to me so he can be as close as he can to me. It's cute and I like it, except...

"Daddy, you're hard," I say, squirming a little and teasing his cock with my butt.

He grinds against me, my bare ass and his pants-covered cock.

"I am, Fiona," he says with a careful grin. "I don't know what you do to me, but you do it really well, baby."

"Daddy?" I say.

"What is it, baby?"

"Can I--" But I don't finish my sentence.

"Can you what?" he asks, helping me.

"I've never... um... I've never done it with anyone before..."

"Done what, baby?" he asks me, a grin on his lips.

"I've never had sex," I say, blushing hard. "I've never had a man's cock inside my tight little pussy before."

"Do you want to try it?" he asks.

He tries to keep a steady tone, but I can sense the excitement in his voice. That, combined with the spanking from before, and I'm wetter than wet. I want Daddy so bad... I want to see if we can be together. I know that doesn't mean we can *"be together"* be together, but I want to know if we can be together like that. I want to know if Daddy fits inside me.

"Please, Daddy?" I ask. "Please. I promise to be a good girl for you. Promise!"

"Oh yeah?" he asks, laughing. "Alright, baby, but... I mean, I'm kind of big, and you've never done this before. I could barely get two fingers inside you earlier, so I don't know if--"

I know. I know I know I know. I really do! But...

I reach behind me and scramble with Daddy's pants. I unzip his zipper and I unbutton them. Daddy helps me and pulls his pants and underwear down, letting them fall to his ankles. I just want to know if Daddy will fit inside me. I need to know. I want his cock to be the first cock I ever feel inside my pussy. I want to know what it's like.

Daddy's hard, too. He's incredibly hard, at least as hard as he was before when he spanked me on his bed and came all over my back and my ass. I hold Daddy's cock for him at first, sliding the head up and down my slit so he can feel how wet and ready I am for him. I don't know if that matters, though. I know I'm wet enough for Daddy, but I'm worried I'm too tight.

I've never done anything like this before, not even by myself with a vibrator or anything, so...

"Alright, baby," Daddy says. "I'm going to go slow. Be a good girl for me, alright? If it's too much, you can tell me, Fiona. I'm just going to--"

I feel the head of Daddy's cock slide past my slick lower lips. He tries to guide himself inside me with his hand, but my pussy clenches instinctively, blocking him. Daddy rubs his cock up and down my slit, teasing me until I calm down a little. Once I'm not clenching as hard, Daddy lines the head of his cock up with my pussy and pushes slowly into me from behind.

It doesn't work at first. I scrunch up my face and grab the sink in front of me.

"Harder, Daddy," I say to him. "You can go harder. Just... just slow, alright? It doesn't hurt, so you can push a little harder. You can be a little rougher with me, Daddy. Please, Daddy, please... I want you inside me..."

Daddy reaches around in front of me while pushing in from behind me. He lays one hand on my hip, pulling me back against him. The other palm rests on my pubis, fingers reaching lower. He slowly strokes my clit, gently easing me into ecstasy. It feels good and I clench tight around the head of Daddy's cock without thinking about it. As soon as I start to clench, Daddy pushes a little harder inside me. He pulls my hip and pushes from behind and plays with my clit, and...

Inch by beautifully agonizing inch, Daddy's cock fits inside me. He's halfway in now and I feel like I'm ready to burst, but I want more. I want to see if Daddy fits all the way inside me.

"Fiona," Daddy says, a rough whisper in my ear. "Baby, I... I don't think we should do this. It feels fucking amazing, but... we can't, baby. I don't want to get you pregnant. I could cum any second. Seriously, Fiona, your pussy is incredible. You have no idea what you're doing to me."

"You feel so good, Daddy," I purr. "You don't have to worry, alright? I'm on birth control. My mom made me start it when I first got my period, so it's fine. You can cum, Daddy. You can cum inside me if you want..."

Which is exactly where this story ends. At least that's what it feels like. Happily ever after? Nope.

Someone knocks on the bathroom door. Yes, with Daddy's cock half inside me, Daddy ready to burst, his fingers expertly playing with my clit, there's someone outside who needs to use the bathroom. Am I the luckiest girl alive or what?

"Fiona? Are you in there?"

Oh shit. It's Emily.

Daddy panics. I panic. He pulls out of me with a popping sound. My pussy stretched to accommodate him, and now I suddenly feel completely empty and like I'm missing something. Which I am. I'm missing Daddy's cock and his cum inside me. I'm missing it so bad!

Daddy's already pulling up his pants. He looks at me, then to the bathroom door, and back at me.

"Yeah, um... hold on!" I say. "I'll be right out!"

"Sure," she says. "Hey, do you know where Grey went? There's no one in the men's bathroom."

"I... nope! I have no idea whatsoever!" I say, looking right at Emily's older brother. "He's not in here, for sure!"

"Well, yeah, Fiona," Emily says, the eye roll obvious even just by hearing her voice. "Why would he be in there?"

"Ummmm..." That's a really good question and I don't know how to answer it.

"Hurry up, alright? I really need to use the bathroom. I'm going to go see if the guy up at the front has seen Grey quick. Make sure no one comes in the bathroom before I get back. I really need to pee!"

"Sure thing!" I say.

And that's it. Kind of? I mean, I don't want it to be it.

"I need to leave before she gets back," Daddy says to me.

"We can go in the men's room," I say to him. "Don't leave me, Daddy. We can go in the men's room and we can finish in there and you can cum inside me."

"Fiona..."

"Please?" I whimper.

"Listen, baby... I..."

Daddy froze while me and Emily were talking. He has

his pants mostly on, but his erection is still throbbing and looks like it's barely going to fit back in his pants, if it even does fit. Might as well keep it out then, right? I know where Daddy can keep it so it'll be all nice and cozy...

"I'm glad that you were my first," I tell him, truthful. "Thank you, Daddy."

He thrusts his cock back into his pants, wincing. Forceful, he buttons and zips his pants back up. Then he pulls me into a hug. He squeezes me tight and holds me close.

"I care about you so much, Fiona," Daddy says, his words soft and nice. "I don't want to ruin our relationship. I liked that, and I love you, but I don't know if I can give you what you want and what you need. It's not just because of Emily. I shouldn't have come in here, Fiona. I think we both know that, right?"

I nod and hold him. My bottom lip quivers and I want to cry, but I need to be strong for Daddy. He's not wrong or anything. It hurts, and I know what I want, but Daddy's not wrong about this. I don't want to lose him, either. And I don't want to hurt Emily.

I just want to be with Daddy...

GREY

Once everything's all clear and I'm sure Emily isn't waiting outside the bathroom door, I make a hasty escape. Let's be honest with each other, too; I don't feel very good about myself at the moment. I get it, and maybe you get it by now, but what do you think this would look like to everyone else in the restaurant.

I mean, it's not like anyone saw me. I sure as fuck hope no one heard me. Or Fiona. Remember this?

"You can be a little rougher with me, Daddy. Please, Daddy, please... I want you inside me..."

Yeah... I do, too...

The pain from having blue balls can't hold a candle to the shame and regret I feel right now. I'm still turned on by everything Fiona said, every fucking thing she is. I just have no fucking clue why I'm doing this to myself, or to her, or to anyone. What do you think Emily would say if she found out?

I love Emily. She's my sister, and we're basically the only family we have left. We've been there for each other for twelve years. Through everything. Absolutely everything, and it's like...

I don't know. I have no clue, Emily. I don't know why Fiona turns me on so much. I don't know why I love hearing her call me Daddy. I don't know why I want to spank her ass and tell her she's been naughty and then to cuddle the fuck out of her and call her Daddy's good girl.

Every time it happens, it feels perfect. It feels right. It's like I know exactly what I've been missing all my life.

And then my sister comes knocking at the bathroom door while I'm slowly trying to fit my cock as far into Fiona's pussy as I can. That's a real great and quick way to snap yourself back to the reality of the situation, let me tell you.

I hide out in the men's restroom for a few, just waiting this whole thing out. Don't mind me. I hear Fiona and Emily talking in the hall outside the bathrooms for a second, and then Emily heads in while I guess Fiona goes back to our table. I keep waiting for a few minutes, which turns into longer than I intended.

Emily's out of the bathroom by the time I leave. Slow and completely unsure of myself, I walk down the hall, head back into the main dining area and to our table. My chicken florentine awaits. And, you know, Emily and Fiona are there, too.

Fiona glances up at me with this shy, sort of innocent look. There's a piece of pasta hanging out of her mouth, and I'm tempted to just *Lady and the Tramp* that shit. Grab the end, pop it into my mouth, and we both join up in the middle, you know? I want to kiss Fiona so fucking bad right now it hurts.

Fiona sucks the piece of pasta into her mouth and ruins any chance I had at my grand romantic gesture. To be honest, I'm not sure *Lady and the Tramp* is the movie I should go to for grand romantic gestures in the first place, though. Maybe it's for the best.

Emily chomps down on a ravioli, chews, and swallows. She gives me a dirty look when I sit down and start eating my chicken florentine without saying a word.

"Really, Grey?" Emily asks me. "Really?"

Wait. Fuck. Did Fiona tell her everything? Holy shit. I can't do this right now. I can't fucking--

"Where were you?" my sister asks.

"Uh, in the bathroom?" I say, playing it cool. "What's it to you?"

"I knocked on the door!" she says, accusing me of something. I don't know what yet, though.

"Yeah?" I say. Still cool. Totally fucking chill over here.

"Yup! I did!"

"I thought I heard something. I didn't realize it was you. I just figured someone was stumbling around in the hall. Sorry, Emily. I was kind of distracted, so..."

"What were you doing?" she asks, giving me the evil eye.

"Do you really have to ask what I was doing in a bathroom? What do you think people do in the bathroom?"

Uh huh. Keep at it, Grey. You can do this.

"I don't know," Emily says, tossing her shoulders up. "I just don't know! You and Fiona have both been acting odd ever since we got here. It's strange. It's really peculiar."

"Peculiar?" I ask. "What is this, *Alice in Wonderland?* Who even says that?"

"I know what's wrong," Emily says, somber. "You guys don't have to hide it from me anymore. That just makes it worse. I'm upset enough about it as it is."

Fuck. Seriously, she knows. What else can that mean? I'm pretty sure Fiona has the same thought as me because her eyes go wide and she looks at Emily like she's about to bring doom and destruction upon us all. I wouldn't even doubt it. I love my sister and all, but I feel like she's one of those girls that seems cute and sweet but could go crazy on you at any second. Like, straight up jab an ice pick in your tires.

I don't know why I feel that way. She's never jabbed an ice pick in anyone's tires. As far as I know, she's never actually done anything crazy, either. I just like to think that once my sister gets a boyfriend, if he does anything to hurt her, she'll slash his tires and throw a flaming bag of dog shit onto the welcome mat on his front porch. She's a badass like that.

So yeah, like I said, Fiona and I are done. Caught in the act. Emily won't let us out of this. It's over. I'm going to get yelled at by my sister and she's never going to talk to me again, and...

"I know it's hard, guys. You don't have to pretend like you aren't upset. I'm going away to college and I'm going to miss both of you, too. I'll come back a lot, though. Like, maybe every weekend? And you two can come visit me, too! Right, Daddy? I was talking with Fiona about it earlier and I think it'd be a lot of fun. You could still do work while you're there, and Fiona and I could hang out at my college, and it's not like we'll be that far away. It's only about an hour drive, right?"

My sister doesn't know. She's completely oblivious.

I don't know if that's good or bad.

FIONA

I hate everything that's happening right now.

I hate that Daddy's cock isn't inside me anymore. I don't know which is worse, either. Do I hate the fact that his cock isn't inside me, or is it even worse that I know how it feels to have his cock inside me? Maybe if I never knew, I wouldn't be thinking about this, but now that I've felt it, now that I can remember exactly how it feels, it's...

And that's just *one* thing, but it's not *everything*. Don't worry, there's a lot more that I hate right now, too.

I hate that I've never talked to Emily about this. The first time I ever went over her house to do homework, and then I saw her brother, Grey, I thought he was super hot. Like, there's plenty of guys that are hot, you know? But Grey is super hot. The more I got to know him, the hotter he was, until, um...

I just never told her, and I hate it. When was I supposed to do it, though? That first afternoon when we were working on homework? Oh, yeah, by the way, Emily, your brother is super hot. I want him to take my virginity, please and thank you.

Um, no. Who even does that? And so I hid it from her, but then it got worse, and now I'm eighteen and I call him Daddy and I don't even know what that means anymore. I've never had a Daddy, so Grey is the only thing I can ever imagine when I think of the word. I just...

And I hate that dinner is over. I need to go home now. Emily and Daddy are leaving early in the morning to drive to her new college. I also hate that Emily's going away to college, since it means I won't have a good reason to spend more time with Daddy in the future. At least not as much as I'd like.

As if that wasn't enough, my phone rings when we walk outside.

"Um, hold on," I say to Daddy and Emily. "It's my mom. Just give me a second."

I step away to the side of the building. I don't know why, but I never feel like I can talk to my mom in public, at least not in front of anyone. I go to the back of the restaurant parking lot to a grassy area with a small picnic table. I'm not sure why the table's here because no one ever uses it, but I think it'd be nice to have a candlelit dinner out here one night. With Daddy. Which is never going to happen, so...

I accept the call from my mom. "Hi, Mom. We just finished dinner. Emily's dad is going to bring me home in a second."

"Oh, Fiona, no, that's not a good idea right now, darling," my mom says. "You can't come home tonight."

"Um, what?" I say, confused. "Mom, where am I supposed to go?"

"We've talked about this," my mom says. "You're out of high school now. When are you going to find a job? Tony's been staying over a lot more lately and things are getting serious. You're an adult now, so it makes sense for you to find your own place, doesn't it?"

"Yeah, um... I mean, I get that, and I'm looking for a job, but... Mom, I don't have anywhere to stay right now. I just went out for dinner. I didn't even pay for it. I'm not out here wasting your money or anything. I've been looking for a job basically every day and I've been trying to go in for interviews but it's kind of hard considering I don't even have a college degree and I'm just out of high school. I promise I'll look for an apartment or something once I get a job, though."

"Fiona," my mom says, sounding annoyed and disappointed at the same time. "What do you think's going to happen later in life? What happens if you have a job but it doesn't pay enough for you to get an apartment? What then? You can't keep relying on me forever. Think of this as a test drive. Figure out a place to stay for tonight and then we can talk about what you're going to do in the future tomorrow."

"Mom, I--"

She interrupts me before I can say anything else, though. "I don't think it's appropriate, either," she says. "I've seen how Tony looks at you when he thinks I'm not looking, Fiona. He's a man, so it's not like I can blame him, but it's just not a good situation for any of us. I think he's the one this time, and I don't want to lose him because you like parading yourself around the house in inappropriate clothes. I've never said anything before, but seriously, Fiona."

"Mom, I... what? I don't even have inappropriate clothes. I have some jeans and t-shirts and I guess I've got a few pairs of shorts. I have no idea what you're talking about. Anyways, it's not me you have to worry about! Tony's the one that--"

"Enough!" my mom says, refusing to listen. "That's absolutely enough of your back talk. Find somewhere to stay tonight, and then we can talk about you staying with me afterwards, but I'm going to be honest with you and say that I need you to be out of the apartment within a week. And I don't want you around when Tony's here. I'm not going to put up with it, Fiona. You've done this before and you've ruined my past relationships, so this is it. I'm putting my foot down this time."

I don't even say anything. How can I? When my mom called me I answered just to tell her I'd be home soon. Now I don't even have a home. I don't even have so much as a car I can sleep in for the night, so...

"Goodbye, Fiona," my mom says. "I hope you're in a better mood tomorrow. You're lucky Tony is out getting pizza for our date night. I could have just texted you, but I thought you deserved a phone call at the very least. I'm going to get ready now. Tony's going to work early in the afternoon tomorrow, so you can come back after he leaves.

Don't come by before then. I repeat, do not show up when Tony is here. I'm warning you."

I hang up. I'm not going to say goodbye to someone like her. I kind of always knew my mom was insane, but I didn't realize how far it went. I've definitely never led any of her boyfriends on. I think Tony is a fat, disgusting slob who thinks he's more attractive than he is just because he used to play baseball back in high school.

And since then? Um, yeah, he hasn't done anything. He's just gotten overweight, he's balding, and he has some shitty job as a car salesman at some used car lot in another town. I don't even hate car salesman or anything, and I need to get a car soon so I'll probably be talking to one, but I'd never go to someone like Tony. You should see the reviews his car dealership gets on Yelp! It's pretty bad, and I think there's a lawsuit against them or something, but Tony tells my mom it's all bullshit and sour grapes.

Which is great, but it doesn't help me right now. It doesn't help me to think about how shitty of a person Tony is, and it doesn't help me to think of how shitty my mom is, too. Kicking me out of the house because Tony wants to stare at my ass? What the fuck!

I'm trying not to cry as I head through the parking lot back to where Daddy and Emily are waiting in his car. Except they aren't waiting there, they're just a few feet away from me. When I turn around, I nearly crash into Daddy. I want to, too. I want to crash into his chest and cry and I want him to wrap his arms around me and hold me and tell me what a good girl I am. And I want Emily to understand. I don't want her to hate me. I...

"What happened?" Emily asks me. "Is everything alright, Fifi?"

"Yeah," I say, wiping a tear from my eyes before it has a chance to roll down my cheek. That's it. Just one tear. No more. I refuse. "It's just my mom. Something happened so I can't come home tonight. It's... it's a pipe or something. It broke. And the electricity went out so they're fixing that, and... um..."

Daddy smiles softly at me. I can tell by the look in his eyes that he doesn't believe my lies. Emily looks worried, too, and I doubt she believes me, either.

"You can stay with us tonight," Daddy says. "You're always welcome in our home, Fiona."

"Uh huh. Yup!" Emily says, smiling wide. "We can have a sleepover! It'll be like one last sleepover before I go to college, except we can't stay up late since Daddy and I have to leave early in the morning. Except... maybe Fiona can come with us?" she adds with a sidelong glance towards Daddy.

"Maybe..." he says with a smirk. "Let's take everything one step at a time. I'm sure Fiona has things she needs to do, too."

"Yeah," I say, sniffling. "Kind of. I... I really need to find a job. To pay rent, because... I think it's time for me to move out on my own, you know? I need to find a place first, too."

"Oh," Emily says, with this deviously suspicious look in her eyes. "Well, since my room's going to be empty, I bet you could stay there? If Daddy's alright with it, that is."

"Uhhhh..." Daddy says.

And I'm in complete agreement with him, except also I think I'd love that. Living with Daddy? Yes, please! I promise I'll be a good girl, Daddy. Super extra pinky promise forever, even!

"You're going to get lonely without me," Emily says to Daddy, placing her hands on her hips. "What else were you even going to do with my room? It's not like Fiona won't pay rent. She will as soon as she gets a job. Right, Fiona?"

"Uh huh," I say. "I'm working really hard to find a job, Daddy."

And before I find a job, I bet I can find another way to repay you, Daddy. With kisses, and blowjobs, but I've never given anyone a blowjob, and if I'm a bad girl you can spank me, or we can do yoga together, even naked yoga, and you can put your cock inside me and cum inside me, and...

I think I'm starting to drool or I look really out of it, because Emily comes and gives me a hug, reassuring me.

"It's alright, Fiona," she says, squeezing me tight in her arms. "You don't have to lie, either. Whatever happened with your mom, I'm here for you. We're both here for you. Right, Daddy?"

Daddy nods, but he's kind of staying out of it. Emily refuses to let him, though. She grabs his arm and tugs him over for a group hug.

Daddy's strong, muscular arms wrap around me. They wrap around Emily, too, but I love that he's holding me right now. I love everything about this.

I love you, Daddy...

I know we can't be together, and I know that I can't tell Emily about what happened. I won't. Promise! I'll still be a good girl for you, though. I won't cause any trouble. Not even a little bit.

I'm going to try not to, at least. I really do promise.

GREY

Holy shit, what the fuck have I gotten myself into?

I can't. I can't even fucking do this shit. Except I *have* to. I can't *not* do it. It's like...

Emily and I were talking about everything we had planned for the next morning. She's all packed, so that one's easy. There's a few things I need to put in the car to bring with us, but for the most part we just have to get ready in the morning and then go. It's not that far of a drive, so we can stop off somewhere for breakfast on the way.

I'll help her unpack once we get there, too. It's her freshman year of college, so she needs to live in the dorms with a roommate. She's never met the girl, so that one's going to be hard, but I figured maybe we can all go out to lunch or something. If her roommate's parents are around then we could all spend the day getting to know each other. It'll make this a ton easier, and then I won't have to worry about Emily as much, either.

That's the plan, at least. I just wanted this to be simple, you know? Real fucking straightforward, except...

"Fiona's taking awhile. Do you think we should go check on her?" Emily asks.

Which we do. We did that. And as soon as I turn the corner to where Fiona's talking on the phone with her mother, I see a teary-eyed girl with the most abandoned, lonely look on her face. Fiona stands there, trying to hide her tears, trying to act strong, but it doesn't matter. I've already seen it. I already know what she's really feeling.

So, that's how I ended up back at my house with two teenage girls squealing at each other and giggling constantly. Don't get me wrong, I don't regret it or anything. I wouldn't have left Fiona to fend for herself. It's just that I'm trying to do work in the living room and it's kind of difficult with the two of them doing who knows what in Emily's room right above me.

I guess technically it's up the stairs and behind me, but I'm not an architect and I don't want to get into the physics of it. I can hear them laughing and doing girly shit up there, and it makes it hard to concentrate.

I do some minor, easy work while they're cackling away like a flock of crows or whatever. Eventually things die down, though. They go to sleep at a reasonable time, which is completely unexpected. When have you ever known two eighteen year old girls to go to bed before three in the morning? Because, yeah, let me tell you about all the times when Fiona's stayed over and she and Emily didn't go to bed until three in the morning. This is why my bedroom is on an entirely different floor completely across the house from Emily's.

That's not actually why, but I'm going to pretend it is. Just give me this one. I need it.

It's barely past nine now and they're both quiet, so I guess they're sleeping. Good. We need to leave early in the morning and I don't want to deal with a tired, grumpy Emily. I guess she can sleep in the car on the drive to her college, but I still don't want to deal with it.

I'm working on my computer, vaguely listening to some TV show I left on, and getting work done, when I hear someone creeping around upstairs. Tiptoes, little scampering, barely anything. The house is kind of older and the floors are wood, so things creak sometimes. I listen to the soft, gentle creaks as they trail from Emily's room to the bathroom at the top of the stairs.

Which is fine. People go to the bathroom. I get that, but...

After a little while, the creaking and tiptoeing starts up again. This time they're coming down the stairs. One step at a time, *creak creak creak*, like a sneaky little mouse. So I immediately know it's not Emily. She's about as sneaky as an elephant.

I act like nothing's going on, because I'm pretty sure I don't want to deal with this right now. I can't deal with it. I just can't do this. I...

Fiona sits down on the couch with me without saying a word. She sneaks a peek over at me as she sits at the complete opposite end of the couch. I glance towards her, raising one eyebrow, but she doesn't look at me for long. Instead, she starts watching TV, silent. She pulls her legs up on the couch cushion and tucks them under her butt, then leans onto the armrest.

This is all about as innocuous as anything can get, so I decide to ignore her. I go back to work, reading through some reports, typing a few words here and there, adding some ideas as I go. The TV show keeps playing and eventually it goes to a commercial break.

Fiona looks over at me again and I glance towards her. She smiles shyly and I kind of smile back at her, but like I said before, I can't do this. I think you know what it is that I can't do, and I just can't do it.

So I try to go back to what I'm doing. This works for awhile, but the next time a commercial comes on and I put my laptop on the coffee table to take a quick break, I get a lapful of something else.

Fiona crawls across the couch and sneaks into my lap. She's like a goddamn cat or something. Just plants her butt in my lap, nothing doing, and leans over so she can rest on the other armrest. She started with her own armrest and now she's stealing mine. What the fuck is up with that?

"Excuse me," I say. "What do you think you're doing?"

"Daddy, can we cuddle?" Fiona asks.

She says it in the most innocent way. I'm being completely serious right now. It's so innocent and sweet and adorable. It's all those things, except as soon as she says it my cock starts to twitch. She's not even doing anything weird, either. She's not grinding her ass in my lap, trying to get a rise out of me. She doesn't call me "Daddy" in that seductive way she's so good at.

Nah. It's just cute and sweet and innocent Fiona and for some fucked up reason this turns me on. Why? What the fuck did I ever do to deserve this?

"Do you think that's a good idea?" I ask her. I don't trust myself enough to answer my own question right now.

"Yes," she says, kissing me on the cheek. "I do."

Well, what the fuck? I can't argue with her. I don't have the willpower. When the TV show comes back on after a commercial break I just sit there, Fiona in my lap, and we watch TV together. I'm not even sure what show it is and I kind of missed what happened before this, but it seems alright.

While watching the show, I realize I have nowhere to put my hands. What do normal people do with their hands? Fuck if I know. I kind of fidget trying to figure this out. Fiona sees me and she takes one of my hands and wraps it tight around her stomach. She pulls my other hand away from me and puts it on her hip.

At least she's not wearing something like those yoga pants from before. No, she's got pajama pants instead. They're not Emily's, so that's a plus. We bought Fiona some sleepover clothes awhile back since sometimes she'd stay the night unexpectedly. These are those, and there's nothing innately wrong with them.

I say that, but I still find them kind of sexy. The pink and black plaid pajamas hang loose on her legs. They're tighter by her hips, but they still kind of hang low a little. One small tug could bring them down easily, and then what? Listen, I have no idea if Fiona wears panties with her pajamas. I've never asked, and I'm not about to. I'd be lying if I said I wasn't thinking about it a lot right now, though...

Fuck.

Her top! Let's just go to that, alright? Leave me alone. It's a longsleeve black top with buttons in the front. She could probably wear it as a regular shirt. Actually, now that I think about it, why didn't she wear this for yoga? This would have been a whole lot easier if she'd just come down in her pajama pants instead of wearing Emily's yoga outfit that's two sizes too tight.

I'm probably lying to myself. None of this is easy. I doubt anything could make it easier.

"Daddy?" Fiona asks, looking up at me. She sits cuddled in my lap, her head resting on my shoulder.

"Yeah?" I answer her.

"I know I can't live here. You don't have to worry. I didn't want to say anything in front of Emily, and I know you wouldn't say anything either, but I know. I'm going to look for an apartment as soon as I find a job, so don't even worry about me, alright?"

The way she says it hurts. I don't know why, it just does.

"You can stay here, Fiona," I say. "If you can find a job, you can stay here. We can figure something out. I'm not going to let you stay without paying rent, though. We need to... uh... it needs to be professional, alright? A professional relationship. We can discuss the specifics later, but I can be reasonable. I'll work with you and help you save, but you can put some money towards the utilities or something. Electric bill, or cable and internet. We'll figure it out."

"What if I can't pay you one month, though?" she asks, giving me a worried look. "Will you have to spank me, Daddy?"

You know what? Yeah, maybe. I shouldn't admit this. I don't even want to spank her for that. I want to spank her for a lot of reasons right now, but none of them involve rent.

"Fiona," I say to her, somehow finding the strength to proceed. "Stop. We can't do that. That can't happen again."

She pouts at me and looks away. "Fine! I was just kidding anyways."

"Why's your mother kicking you out?" I ask her. "What happened tonight?"

She doesn't answer me for awhile. When she does, all she says is, "It's stupid."

"If you did something wrong, you can tell me," I say to her. "I won't get mad. I just want to know how I can help you."

Fiona scoffs and snaps her head towards me. It almost feels like she's about to slap me, but I can tell it's not me that she wants to slap. She furrows her brow and opens her mouth to speak, but the words come out in a huge, incomprehensible mess.

"One word at a time," I remind her, gently patting her hip.

She fidgets and nestles into my lap, the look of pain and anguish slowly easing off of her face.

"I didn't do anything wrong," she says softly. "My mom told me not to come home because her boyfriend keeps staring at me. It's gross. I've never done anything to make him think I like it. I don't even want to talk to him. This isn't the first time it's happened, either. One time my mom went to the store to get some milk for breakfast and I came out wearing my regular clothes for school. I wasn't in anything weird, Daddy. Promise."

She hesitates for a second, but then continues. "He just kept staring at me over the kitchen table. I made myself some oatmeal and he stared at me while I ate it, so I asked him what he's staring at, and he says... he says my breasts look hot in my shirt. All the boys at my school must want to get into my pants. I tell him that's not true, and I'm not like that, and he says that he knows it's true, because that's how he feels, and if I want to while my mom is gone he can show me what it's like to be with a man, and... I ate my oatmeal in my room after that. I locked the door and I heard him try to open it, but he couldn't, and then my mom came home. I... I don't know, Daddy. I didn't do anything, I swear. I never told my mom about that, but she started giving me dirty looks after, and then a couple weeks later he was gone and she had a new boyfriend. It doesn't happen with all of them, but..."

I want to speak, to say words, but I have something stuck in my throat. I choke a little until I finally manage to say, "Baby... it's not your fault..."

"I know, but I'm sorry, Daddy," she says, pushing her

face into my chest. "I'm sorry for teasing you. I promise I didn't tease them like that. I know I shouldn't tease you. I just... I really like you, and you're so nice to me, and Emily's so lucky to have you. I like Emily and she's my friend which makes this so hard for me, because... I don't know. I'm sorry, Daddy. I really am."

"What are you sorry about, baby?" I ask her.

"I'm sorry if you think I'm a bad girl," she says. "I know I'm bad sometimes. Maybe I tease you sometimes when I shouldn't. Just you, though. I... I wouldn't do that with anyone else."

"I know," I tell her, smiling and kissing her hair. "You're not bad, Fiona. You're a good girl. You're wonderful, and Emily loves you. You two are best friends."

"I know, but how can I be friends with her when I want you to make love to me, Daddy?" Fiona asks.

Well, that's a question alright. Yeah...

"You'll find someone," I tell her, trying to stay strong. "You'll find a boy your age who is everything you want, and he'll be there for you, and he'll protect you, and you'll love him so much that when you two finally decide it's time, you'll have the most wonderful and amazing experience together. You'll--"

"I did find him, Daddy," she says. "He's not my age, but he's all of those things, and he's been there for me and protected me without ever trying to tell me that I should have sex with him because of it. He doesn't make me feel like I should do it or that I have to, and I love him, and--"

"Fiona..." I say, my voice rough.

"Daddy? Will you take me to your bed? Just this once?

Just tonight? Please, Daddy? I need you. I just... I need to know what it's like to feel loved, Daddy. Not just friendship or like family, but I need to know everything. If you don't want to, I understand, but I've been a good girl for you for so long and I just..."

FIONA

Daddy wraps me in his arms and picks me up like a princess. He carries me like that, cradled against his chest, and brings me to his bedroom. The door is open, so he steps inside with me and then places me gently on his bed. I lay there, curled up, looking into his eyes with a little bit of wonder and a lot of excitement.

"Fiona, we really shouldn't do this," Daddy says.

"I know, Daddy," I tell him. "I really want to, though."

"I'm going to try and convince you otherwise," he says, smirking at me.

"Is that why you brought me to your bed?" I ask him with a grin.

"Uh... sort of..." he says. "Don't get the wrong idea. I just thought this conversation was better to have in private. I don't think either of us wants Emily to hear us if she goes to the bathroom or wakes up and sees you're not in her room."

"Oh," I say, trying to hide my disappointment.

"Hold on," Daddy says. "I'm going to change for bed quick."

Daddy goes into his private bathroom and closes the door. I don't hear him lock it, but I'm not about to sneak in on him again. My butt still hurts from earlier, and while it's a sexy kind of hurt, I don't know if I can take any more punishment right now. I'm trying to be a good girl, too!

I would really like it if Daddy comes out with no clothes on, though. Because maybe that's how he sleeps? I don't know. It's his room and I've never been in here at night before. Maybe Daddy sleeps naked and then he wakes up with an erection and his cock is all hard and throbbing and beautiful and I want to wrap my fingers around it and stroke him until he cums like he did before.

He came all over my back then, but if he wakes up and we do that he could cum all over my chest instead. Daddy can cum on my breasts and my stomach, or I can open my mouth and try to catch some on my tongue. And we can...

Daddy comes out of the bathroom wearing a pair of loose pajama pants and a t-shirt. It's basically the same kind of thing I have on, but for men. As much as I thought I'd rather see him naked, um... his pajamas kind of turn me on, too. He just looks so casual and confident, and also if he has pajama pants on it's fun because I can slip my fingers into the waistband and tug them down to see what kind of surprise he has for me underneath them. I can't do that if he's naked, now can I? Nope!

I watch him with interest as he walks across the room and comes back to join me. He stands next to me while I lay on his bed staring up at him. After a few moments like that, he shakes his head and grins.

"Are you going to move over so I can get in bed or what?" he asks.

"Oh!" I say, surprised. It's a good surprise, though! I like it. I hurry to scoot over so Daddy can get in bed with me. "There you go, Daddy."

He lays next to me. We aren't touching, but I like this a lot. I like the idea of laying in bed with Daddy, and also maybe sleeping in bed with him. And other things, if I'm being honest. I want to reach over and touch him, but I don't think I can do that. Or I shouldn't do it, at least. A part of me wonders if Daddy would stop me, though? Maybe not, but that doesn't mean it's a good idea.

"Fiona, I'm too old for you," Daddy says. "You're young and you need to enjoy life."

"You aren't that old, Daddy," I say to him, laughing. "You're only thirty."

"Yes, but that doesn't change the fact that I've got a lot more life experience. I don't want to take advantage of you."

"I don't even think you could take advantage of me if you tried," I say, truthful. "You're not like that."

"What happens if we do it?" he asks me. "Let's just say that we don't stop ourselves and we just go for it. We have sex, and maybe it's great. Maybe it's not. That part doesn't matter. What happens if it doesn't work out and then it makes things hard between you and Emily. Are you going to stop being her friend? I don't want that, Fiona. Or what happens if it makes things hard for me and Emily? I don't want to hurt my sister, and I don't want to hurt you, either."

"Maybe..." I say, because he has a point. "What happens if none of that happens and we're supposed to be together and we're soulmates, though?"

"Fiona..." Daddy says with a sigh.

"I already love you," I tell him. "I'm sorry, but I do. I can't help it. I loved you even before today, and after everything that happened I can't stop thinking about you. I know you're Emily's, and that's special, but I want you to be mine and I want us to have something special but in a different way."

"I... I love you, too, Fiona, but... I don't know if it's right. I don't know if I love you the way you want me to love you. I'll help you with anything, and I care about you a lot, but that's different from a passionate love or a romantic love. There's a lot of different kinds of love, Fiona. It's not all the same."

"I know that," I tell him. "I just... I know about the other kind of love, and I thought that was it, but I think you're wrong about it always being different. I mean, yeah, it's different, but I saw you being passionate earlier, Daddy. I felt it, too. When you spanked me, and then you were telling me to be a good girl, and when you made me cum, and then afterwards when we were at the restaurant and you came into the bathroom. That was really hot and passionate."

"I shouldn't have done any of that," he says. "You shouldn't have come into the bathroom, either. You shouldn't have teased me while we were doing yoga. I have no idea what Emily was thinking letting you traipse around in clothes like that. It doesn't matter if the three of us were alone in the house. I can't even begin to--"

"Do you think you could love me in a romantic way?" I ask, interrupting him. "I mean, do you think you could go on a date with me, and fall in love with me like that, and I know it's a different kind of love, but could you love me both ways? Or all three ways, I mean. Could you, um..."

Unconditional love. Passionate love. Romantic love.

I just want Daddy to love me and to never leave me, but to be with me, and to hold me. I want him to spank me if I do something wrong, but to be loving and caring about it, and then to cuddle me after. I want him to bring me up, so very high up, and show me the passion and wonder that he's gained through his experiences in life, but I want to give him some of my innocence and let him know that he can be whoever he wants to be when he's with me, just like he's always been.

He can be my Daddy, and that's alright, and I'll be his good girl, and Emily can be my friend, and he can be her Daddy but in a different way, and it's not wrong or bad, and I don't want Emily to hate me, and I don't want to hurt her by loving Daddy the way I do, and...

"I think we need to stop and have this conversation later," Daddy says quietly.

"Why?" I ask him. "Did I say something wrong? I didn't mean to."

"No, it's..." He hesitates. "You didn't say anything wrong, Fiona. I just don't know if I can do this right now. I was planning on trying to convince you that we can't do this, but every time I hear you talk and say more and answer my questions, or when you ask questions of your own, it's... it's too hard."

"What's too hard?" I ask him, rolling onto my side and resting my head on my hands, watching him.

He looks at me for a few seconds, then stops and stares at the ceiling.

"This," he says. "Everything. I wanted to convince you this was a bad idea, and I still think it is, but you're starting to convince me I might be wrong and that we should do it. The thing is, if we do, we can't go back. We can't act like it never happened. I know what happened today, and I never wanted to cross that line. It's already hard enough as it is. I don't know if I can handle more than that. I don't even know if I can handle what already happened."

I listen, and I understand, but the only thing I keep hearing over and over again in my mind is:

"You're starting to convince me I might be wrong and that we should do it."

Yes, please...

GREY

I really should kick Fiona out of my bed. Or else I should go sleep on the couch. I don't know why I'm still here. I'm not here for me. That's what I keep telling myself. Fiona is vulnerable right now. Can you blame her? After everything that happened with her mother and after what she told me earlier, I sure can't.

It's not much, but my parents were alive until I was eighteen. At least I had that, and every day I wish I had more, but I'm still grateful for what I do have. I have Emily, and we have each other. I'm alive, I've managed to become successful in the face of adversity, and now that Emily's eighteen I can stop worrying about her as much.

I'm still going to worry, though.

While I grew up with our parents, Emily only really ever grew up with me. She remembers our mom and dad a little bit, but it's hard when you lose parents at such a young age. That's what everyone tells me, but I wouldn't really know.

As for Fiona...

She never had a father, and I don't know if she really had a mother, either. I didn't know what I was getting into. I didn't know what it meant to be her Daddy. It's nothing like I ever could have imagined, and if I'm being really fucking honest with you right now it scares me.

"Daddy" means more to her than I thought possible. It's not about being a father. It's not even being a father figure. It's like being *everything*. How can I even begin to be something like that to someone?

Why am I so tempted to try to be exactly that for her?

These thoughts are killing me. I can't take it anymore, so I'm about to give up and either kick Fiona out of my room or go sleep on the couch. I need to do something.

When I turn around to tell her, she's sleeping, though. She has her hands under her cheek, hands and head resting on one of my pillows. Mouth open slightly, she breathes softly while she dreams. I feel her breath on my face, gentle and sweet. Before I even realize what I'm doing, I press forward and give her a kiss on the cheek.

Her eyes flutter open a little, sleepy, and she yawns and looks at me.

"Sorry I fell asleep, Daddy," Fiona says, mumbling.

"It's alright, baby," I tell her. "You can sleep here tonight. I think it's better if I go sleep on the couch, though. I'll set an alarm and wake up early and then wake you up so Emily won't find out you slept down here."

"Nooooo..." she says, sleep and dreams in her voice. "Don't sleep on the couch."

"Do you want me to bring you back upstairs?" I ask.

"I'll carry you, but we need to be quiet. We can't wake up Emily."

"Nooooooooooo, not that, either," she says, a little grumpy.

It's basically the cutest thing I've ever seen and heard. Her lips pout into an adorable little heart shape, almost like she's kissing the air.

"What do you want to do then?" I ask her, but I'm almost afraid to find out.

"Can we cuddle?" she asks. "Can I sleep here with you, Daddy? And you can set your alarm and we'll wake up early and then Emily won't find out. Promise."

Now, I know what you're thinking. Cuddling? Yeah, that's the least of my concerns. Fiona's almost asleep, and cuddling is probably the most innocent thing I could possibly do with her right now. I mean, when you compare it to what I did earlier, then I think cuddling wins, hands down. I don't think anyone can get mad at me for cuddling with Fiona.

Except, what I haven't told you before now is that I've had an erection for awhile. I thought I had myself under control when I changed into my pajama pants. I usually sleep in them without underwear, so I just sort of tossed them on without thinking about it. Except the more I talked with Fiona, the more I started to realize just how much I wanted to--

It's not just fucking, alright? I mean, yeah, when you get right down to it, I want to fuck her brains out. Not at first. I don't want to hurt her or anything. It took awhile for me to fit my entire cock into her tight, eighteen year old pussy. I feel like a huge fucking pervert for thinking about it like that, but let's be real here. She's eighteen and her pussy is tight as fuck, and yet somehow I managed to thrust my entire cock inside her.

We stopped after that, but like I said, I'd be lying if I tried telling you I didn't want to fuck her brains out. I want to be gentle too, though. I want her first time to be everything she hoped for and more. I want to make her feel so fucking good. I want to be there for her, unconditionally, but I want to fuck her with a passion she could only dream of, and I want to make love to her with all the romance she deserves.

I want to be her Daddy and I want her to be my good girl. I don't care if that makes me fucked up. This girl means so much to me and I'd give her everything she ever wanted if I could.

Now, I'm not saying it's a *good* idea. It's a bad idea. It's a very fucking bad idea. I should not be the one doing this for her, and I know it, but the way she talks about it makes me wonder if I'm wrong and she's right.

I'm not. I don't think I am. I just...

Let's just get back to the matter at hand. She wants to cuddle and my cock is harder than hard. Without underwear, the thing's just tenting the front of my pajama pants, throbbing and pulsing, ready to do something I shouldn't be doing.

Not sure how I'm supposed to cuddle with her like this, you know?

"*Please, Daddy?*" Fiona asks, smiling sleepily at me.

She rolls onto her side with her back to me. It's a classic

spooning position, except I'm kind of facing away from her. Maybe we can do this. If I just, uh...

I move back a little. Back to back, right? We can cuddle like that. I'm not sure that's considered cuddling, but she's tired so maybe she won't notice.

I regret to inform you that she does. She notices immediately.

"That's not how you cuddle," she says, pouty. "You need to turn around."

Alright, cock. You and I need to have a serious conversation. I get that you want to thrust yourself deep inside Fiona's fine as fuck pussy, but we can't be doing that right now. Or ever. So just calm down, alright?

My cock throbs at the thought of Fiona's fine as fuck pussy and doesn't even come close to calming down.

Nevermind. I know what to do. I maneuver carefully, pulling my shaft up so it's trapped in the waistband of my pajama pants. Half my cock sticks out, but it's hidden beneath my shirt, so that's fine. The other half presses tight against my body, pointing up to my chin. This isn't exactly ideal, but at least I don't have to worry about my tenting problem anymore.

I can safely turn around and spoon Fiona without her realizing anything. Except I need to set my alarm, so I have to do that first. I reach for my phone on my bedside table and set an alarm for way too fucking early. After I'm done, I put my phone back and sort of swivel around carefully so I can spoon with Fiona. Need to be careful not to screw up my cockblocking mechanism, you know?

Yes, I'm cockblocking myself. Never thought I'd see the day that happened, but here I am.

Fiona pushes back against me when I finally start to cuddle with her. She lets out a soft moan, which I'm pretty sure is just from being tired, but it sounds sexy as fuck, regardless. My cock twitches at the sound of it, straining hard against my pajama pants waistband. Fiona freezes. Shit. She noticed, didn't she?

She doesn't say anything, though. Just pushes her ass back a little, nestling it in my lap. Is it still a lap if you're laying down? I have no idea. I'm not a linguistics professional. I can't answer questions like that.

I'm fine, though. This is fine. My cock is trapped, she won't realize what's going on, and if I can just make it for a few seconds until she goes to sleep I think I can handle this. I'll just go to sleep, too. Or else I'll sneak off to the bathroom while she's sleeping, take care of myself, and come back with no one being the wiser.

You've got this, Grey. You can do it. I believe.

Sometimes you have to give yourself a mental pep talk, especially when it involves a situation like the one I now find myself in. Just trust me on this one.

I trusted myself, but then something betrayed me. I don't know what it was, either my pajama pants or my cock, but it was one of those.

Fiona shifts around, trying to get comfortable. Unfortunately my pajama pants are in a slightly precarious position right now. With my cock straining hard against the waistband, and me pressed tight against Fiona, some unfortunate things happen, and my pajama pants slide down. My cock slaps hard against her back, freed from the confines of my pants.

And... so... I don't mean to do this, alright? It's just instinctive, and no guy wants their throbbing cock squished up somewhere. It's not like this *specific* situation is the issue, it's just the entire thing in general. I kind of scoot back without thinking about it in order to make myself more comfortable. My cock slaps downwards, jutting straight out between my legs, and the next time Fiona pushes back against me to get more comfortable, my shaft slides between her thighs.

She's wearing pajama pants, so it's not like anything terrible happens. More terrible, I mean. It's not like anything worse than my cock slapping out of my pants and diving between her thighs happens, which is actually pretty terrible now that I think about it. Holy fucking shit.

Admittedly, this is a lot more comfortable than trying to keep my cock trapped in the waistband of my pants or keeping it pressed tight against her back, though. My cock is free, and it's happy about that. I'm not happy, but my cock doesn't give a fuck what I think. It does what it wants.

"Um... *Daddy...*" Fiona says, acting all coy and innocent. "What's this?"

I don't have time to answer before she reaches between her legs and touches my cock. Her fingers tease and toy with the head. I thought I had issues before, but this is on an entirely different level. I don't cum, but my cockhead is already coated in precum and with Fiona playing with me I sort of throb and pulse, shooting out a little more precum. Like a mini-orgasm, I guess? I don't know how to explain this to you. You'd have to be there.

Fiona's there, and let me assure you she's quite pleased with herself. She giggles as a little precum streams directly from my cock to her fingers. She rubs my slickness all around the head of my cock. It feels incredible, but also ridiculously sensitive, and I start to buck and shake. Gentle, she slows down, but this isn't any better. Her nails rake lightly across my slick cock, sending shivers through my body.

"Fiona," I say, trying to be strong. "We can't. We need to stop this."

"I know," she says, smiling.

To her credit, she stops. I guess that's what we're going to call this. She stops playing with the head of my cock and instead she reaches for the waistband of her pajama pants. When she slides them down I soon find out that I'm not the only one who doesn't wear underwear with their pajamas. Good to know, right?

Uh, no. It's not. This is very very bad. Holy shit.

We go back to spooning, or that's what I'm trying to do. My cock is sort of in the way and I'm trying to figure out a way to fix this. Nothing's working, but at least Fiona isn't playing with it anymore. That's the last thought I have before she pushes back against me, grinding her ass in my lap, trying to spoon with me.

Except there's nothing between my cock and her pussy anymore. Absolutely nothing.

The head of my cock lodges in between her lower lips. I'm trapped again, but this time isn't quite the same as before. Instinctive, because I need her so much it hurts, I push forward while she pushes back. Before I know it, inch by delirious inch, my cock sinks into her tight pussy. I'm over halfway in before I realize what's happening and it's a little too late to stop now.

"It's okay, Daddy," Fiona says. "You aren't hurting me. I know what to expect this time and I know how it feels. You feel so good, Daddy. You can just be inside me, alright? We don't have to do anything else. We can just cuddle like this, since it's easier for you. Right, Daddy? If your cock is hard like this then it'll hurt to put it back in your pants. I don't mind if it stays here. You can keep your cock inside me, Daddy..."

I wince at the memory, at the thought I might have hurt her before in the restaurant, but my cock throbs hard inside her, happy to be back. Her pussy clenches tight against my shaft, squeezing me for all I'm worth.

"Did I hurt you earlier, baby?" I ask her. "Did I hurt you in the restaurant? I didn't mean to, but you just... you feel so good, baby. Do you like Daddy's cock inside you like this?"

"Ohhhh, Daddy, I *love* it," she says, purring. "You didn't hurt me, Daddy. It was just different. I didn't know how it would feel. I've always wanted to feel it, but I wanted to wait and I wanted to be with you, Daddy. You're so nice and gentle and... you're very big, Daddy, but I'm happy you fit inside me. It's like my pussy is perfect for your cock, don't you think?"

"Fiona... baby..." I say, torn. "We shouldn't do this, but..."

"Yes, Daddy?"

"Do you want to feel what it's like, baby? To have sex, I mean. You know what it's like to have a cock inside you, but do you want to feel what it's like when it moves? Then we need to stop, alright?"

She hesitates, and I almost think I've gone too far, but after a few seconds she says, "I want to feel it, Daddy. If it's with you, I want to feel it. And if you need to stop after, we can. I trust you, Daddy."

"Alright, baby," I say to her, whispering against the back of her neck. "So... this is how it feels all the way inside. Just like this..."

I wrap my arm around her waist and press my palm onto her stomach. I pull her back onto me while I slowly push the rest of the way inside her. My cock bottoms out, slowly grinding as far into her as I can. I grind a little more, getting a feel for things. She pushes back against me.

"Daddy, that feels really good," she says, giddy. "It's like you're in my tummy almost. I can feel you, like... right here..."

She rests her hands on the back of mine, guiding my palm down her stomach. When she finds the spot, she pushes gently on my hand, pressing it into her stomach a little below her belly button.

"Right there, Daddy," Fiona says. "That's where I feel you..."

I grin and kiss the side of her neck. "Do you want to feel more, baby?"

"Uh huh," she says with a whimper. "Yes, please, Daddy..."

I pull out slowly, and then I slide back in. Once more, and then again. Each time I thrust back into her is easier than the last as my cock forces her pussy to accept me. She grinds back against me as I thrust hard into her. It's a shame I need to stop soon, and I'm finding it harder and harder to remind myself of that.

"This is what it feels like, Daddy?" she asks. "This is what it feels like to make love?"

"Yes, baby," I tell her. "But... sometimes there's a little more. It's not just this. Do you want me to show you?"

"Show me, Daddy," Fiona whispers. "I want you to show me all of what it's like."

Without another word, I move my hand lower down her stomach. I shift a little on my bed until my fingers are in just the right spot. The next time I thrust into her, I start stroking her clit gently. She trembles the first time I do it. The more I tease her clit, the more her legs start to shake.

"And there's kissing, too, baby," I tell her. "You can't kiss me back like this, but I can kiss you. I can kiss your neck... just like this..."

I thrust deep inside her and rub her clit up and down. She grinds back against me and I kiss her neck. I suck gently and then bite lightly on her soft skin.

"Daddy, I... I'm going to..." Fiona pants. "I'm going to cum soon, Daddy. Can I cum? Please? I've been a good girl, Daddy. Promise!"

"You can cum for me, baby," I tell her. "That's a part of making love, too. It's natural. This is what it should feel like."

Once I give her permission, she goes silent. Not

completely because she's still whimpering in pleasure, but she doesn't say anything else. I thrust into her slowly, savoring every aching feeling as her pussy clenches down hard on my cock. She felt amazing before, but actually having sex with Fiona is beyond heaven. I know I'm going to hell for this, but a part of me feels like it's completely worth it.

"Daddy..." Fiona says. "Daddy... daddy, right there... yes. *Yes yes yes*... oh my God, Daddy!"

Fiona's entire body spasms as her orgasm rips through her. Her pussy clamps down on my cock so hard she almost forces me out of her. I thrust in hard and hold myself there, doing everything I can just to keep myself inside her. She bucks and thrashes, her feet kicking up the covers. While I play with her clit, she grabs my wrist, just holding me tight, keeping my hand there. I kiss and suck hard on her neck, letting her enjoy every single second of her first time.

This is seriously the sexiest fucking thing I've ever done. I have never been with a girl like Fiona. I'm not sure I should be, but it happened and I can't change it now. My cock kind of made the decision for me, and I feel like I'm going to regret this later, but for now, I'm completely ecstatic. I need this girl so bad.

"That was so amazing, Daddy..." Fiona says in a daze. "Did you feel it? Could you feel me squeezing your cock?"

"I felt it, baby," I say, smiling. "You liked it? It felt amazing to me, too."

"Did it?" she asks, curious.

"It did. That's what it should feel like. Now you know, right?"

"Uh huh, but... Daddy? What's it feel like if you cum inside me?"

Yeah, I'm dead. I can't do this anymore. I'm going to hell. Fuck.

FIONA

Daddy's cock twitches hard when I ask him what it would feel like if he cums inside me. My pussy grabs onto his shaft, squeezing hard, and he twitches even more. It's like a never ending circle and he twitches and pulses inside me, then my pussy squeezes and grabs onto him. I just had an orgasm but this feels really good, too. I want it. I want more.

"I don't think we should--" Daddy starts to say.

"How will I know, though?" I ask him. "You were teaching me, right? That's all, Daddy. It's not bad. I'm not bad, am I? I'm your good girl, right?"

"You're not bad, baby," Daddy says, shaking his head. "It's just... you shouldn't let someone cum inside you unless you... you need to be serious with them. In a serious relationship. You never know what can happen, and..."

"Daddy, please? Can you please cum inside me so I know what it feels like?"

"Fiona, we really shouldn't be doing this," he says.

"I know," I tell him. "I know, but..."

Daddy thrusts hard into me. His hand moves from my clit to my hip and he holds onto me tight. He pulls out and thrusts back in hard, pulling me against his cock. My body rocks and sways, controlled by Daddy. Everything I do is because of him. I'm his right now. I'm Daddy's good little girl and he's just showing me what it's like. He's just...

"Soon, baby," he grunts. "Daddy's going to cum soon. Daddy's going to cum a lot for you, so you'll know exactly what it's like. Really really soon, baby."

Daddy thrusts into me one more time. Twice. On the third thrust he pounds all the way inside me. His cock twitches and throbs, fast and uncontrollable. I feel like his cock is jumping inside me, and then a half second later I feel his cum. Jet after jet of Daddy's cum pumps into my pussy as his cock twitches over and over again. I squeeze Daddy's cock with my pussy to help him get every last drop of cum into me.

It's warm and nice and I love feeling Daddy inside me like this. I wish I could feel him inside me like this again, but even if this is the only time I like it.

"You came inside me," I say, smiling bright. I can't stop smiling right now.

"Did you feel it, baby?" he asks me. "Could you feel everything, Fiona?"

"Uh huh. I did, Daddy."

"Fiona, I..."

"I know, Daddy," I tell him before he says anything. "I

know we can't do this again. I know. I promise. I won't tell Emily and I don't want to ruin anything, so don't worry. I promise I won't."

Daddy pulls out of me slowly, but he still feels really hard. As soon as his cock is all the way out of me, his cum splashes onto the bed. I don't know why but I didn't even think about that happening. I start to giggle and Daddy laughs, too.

"I think we made a mess," I tell him.

"We'll clean it up," Daddy says, patient. "I'm not done with you yet, though. I need you, Fiona. I've already gone this far, so..."

Daddy flips me onto my back. I gasp, unsure what to expect. I blink fast, once, twice, and after the second time when I open my eyes Daddy's between my legs. His cock is still hard and it looks like he wants to find a good place to put it.

I think I know the perfect place for your cock, Daddy...

"You said you could feel me in your tummy before, baby?" Daddy says. "Let's see how deep I was inside you."

Daddy pushes himself as close to me as he can. His cock bounces onto my stomach, hard and wet from our mixed orgasm. He lays his cock across my stomach and then takes my hand to show me just how far he can fit inside me.

"All the way up to my belly button!" I say, laughing. "Daddy, you're really big!

"It's different inside you, but like this it's definitely up to your belly button," he says, grinning at me.

"What are you going to do now, Daddy?" I ask, grinning back at him.

"Baby... I'm going to keep going until you either tell me to stop or we both pass out because we're exhausted. Just tell me if it's too much and I'll stop, though. Alright?"

"Really?" I ask, eyes wide.

"Of course," he says. "I don't want to hurt you or force you to do anything. I just... you feel so good. You feel amazing and I need more. If you tell me to stop, I'll stop, though. I promise."

"No, um... I didn't mean *that*," I say, giggling. "I meant you're going to keep going until we both pass out?"

"Fiona, don't even fucking tempt me," he says with a smirk. "You're going to regret it."

"Nuh uh!" I say, shaking my head fast. "Put your cock back inside me, Daddy. Please? I want to feel it like this."

Daddy pulls back, lines himself up, and then thrusts his cock deep inside me. I gasp, caught off guard. Oh wow! This is... it's different. I never really thought about it before, but different positions feel a lot different. Daddy couldn't go as deep when he was behind me while we were spooning, but now he can go deeper, and he's touching different spots inside me.

He grabs my hips and lifts me up a little, then thrusts in fast. Oh my God! Even that's different! What the heck! Sex is...

Sex is amazing, but it's because it's with Daddy. It's because he cares about me. It's because he loves me, even if maybe we can't have romantic love, but we have other kinds of loves. I don't know. I just want to feel Daddy right now and I want Daddy to need me. I want to be his good girl.

This isn't like before. It's not making love like Daddy showed me the last time. It's faster and rougher, but I like this a lot, too. Daddy fucks me hard on his bed. He rubs my clit with his thumb and drives me wild while he pounds his cock deep inside me.

"Daddy, I... yes, Daddy, *please*, Daddy..."

I cum for Daddy a second time. Just as I'm cumming, Daddy lets out a roar and drives his cock deep inside me. I tremble and fight against him, my legs and arms flailing on the bed. Daddy pins me in place and forces an orgasm into me, and then he cums hard inside me, too.

Once we're done, he crashes on top of me. I grab his cheeks and kiss his face over and over. I kiss his cheeks and his nose and...

Daddy kisses me back. Our lips touch and it's like magic and softness and everything beautiful in the world. It's like unicorns and rainbows, except maybe more masculine because I don't know how Daddy would feel about that. It's like unicorns and rainbows for me, at least.

"Daddy, I really do love you," I tell him. "You're so nice to me."

"I love you, too, Fiona," he says. "I want to take care of you. I want to..."

"Can we go again?" I ask him, half teasing, and half, um... half serious? *Mhm!*

"Again?" Daddy asks, smirking at me. "You haven't had enough yet?"

"No, *you* haven't," I tell him. "Remember? You told me

you were going to keep going until I asked you to stop or we both passed out, so..."

Daddy leans back and pulls out of me. He stands up a little and then before I know it he grabs my legs and flips me onto my stomach. Lifting my ass into the air, grabbing onto my hips, Daddy drives his cock back into my slick, used pussy. It's Daddy's pussy, for him and him alone. He can use it as much as he likes.

He presses forward, pinning me to the bed with one hand. My breasts shake and bounce against his mattress. I don't know why but I really like this position. It's like I've been a bad girl and Daddy needs to punish me, but I'm also a good girl and Daddy is giving me a present. I thought I would only get one present in the form of Daddy's cock, but then I get two presents.

Daddy reaches around so he can play with my clit while he fucks me hard from behind. His cock feels different inside me again, too. With our combined orgasms, not just one now but two, Daddy's cock slides into me easily. Our bodies slap and squelch together, loud and messy sounding. It gets even worse when Daddy quickly gives me another orgasm. My body betrays me and gives in to him and his fingers and his cock just feel so good.

Daddy doesn't cum immediately after that, though. He makes me cum one more time for him before he fills me up. Right before he cums he presses both palms against the center of my back, pinning my chest to the bed, and then he thrusts hard into me over and over. He doesn't stop thrusting when he comes this time, and his cum splashes and sloshes inside of me and all over his bed, too.

We've made quite the mess, let me tell you...

Really now, Daddy? How are we going to sleep in this bed?

GREY

I can't even think right now. I'm way too tired. I'm exhausted, I somehow managed to cum inside Fiona three times over the course of who the fuck knows how long, and now I'm staring at her sexy ass after I just finished pounding into her from behind.

This ass is everything I've ever dreamed of and then some. Staring at it during yoga earlier? Yeah, that was nice, but staring at it when I'm balls deep inside her pussy is basically what dreams and magic are made of.

Going to be honest, despite how tired I am I kind of want to spank her again. Just a little bit. Not because she needs to be punished, but just because. Maybe a little swat here and there, you know?

Also, I'm about to pass out. I'm not even sure how I'm still awake. What time is it? No, don't answer that. Don't even tell me. I know I have to wake up early to bring Emily to college and now I'm dreading it. What the fuck was I thinking?

I pull out of Fiona then I jump off my bed. I grab her around the waist and just lift her up and off my bed before putting her on the ground. She squirms in my arms and giggles like the sexy fucking nymph she is.

"We need to sleep," I tell her. "No more. I can't."

"*Awwww,*" she says, pouting at me.

"Don't you fucking pout at me, Fiona."

"But... but, *Daddy...*"

"No."

"That's sad."

"You know what's sad? This bed. Look at what you did."

"What! Me?" She pouts at me. "I think you helped, too."

I wave my arms over the bed. What used to be my nice, comfortable bed, is now a mess of wetness caused by my cum and Fiona's orgasms. I really shouldn't complain about this because it's pretty impressive if I do say so myself. And I have sheets and everything so I can change it easily enough. I'm just tired, so...

I stride confidently towards my closet, open it, and pull out a thick blanket. One smooth sweep is all it takes, and the blanket unfurls completely. Like some sort of sex magician, I drape the blanket over my entire bed in a single pass. All together, that whole thing, from closet to unfurling to draping, it all somehow works out perfectly.

Fiona stares at me, eyes wide, clearly impressed.

"Wow," she says. "Daddy, you're amazing."

"That?" I ask her, sighing and shaking my head. "You thought *that* was amazing after everything we just did?"

"I mean, that was amazing too, but in a different way."

"Get your naked ass in bed before I spank it," I tell her. "I'm going to sleep."

"Can I sleep with you?" she asks. "Is it alright?"

I slide onto my bed and then pat the spot next to me. "Come here, Fiona."

She scurries into bed, shy, and then lays down next to me. I reach over to the side of the bed and flick off the light. I usually use the light switch on the wall instead, but I'm too lazy for that right now. We lay together, close, but it's different now.

I don't know what I just did. I don't know why I did it, either. I probably shouldn't have, but...

I wrap my arm around Fiona and hold her tight. She nuzzles against me. We're both naked, just laying on top of the blankets without a care in the world. It's nice enough outside that we don't need anything more than ourselves to keep us warm.

Spooning with her, my cock nestled lightly against her ass, I hold her tight. I gently pat her head and tease her hair, kissing lightly behind her ear. She lets out a soft moan and presses tight against me, satisfied.

"I hope you know what a good girl you are," I tell her. "You really are amazing, Fiona."

She melts in my arms. She melts my heart, too. I can barely take this, but I want more of her.

"Thank you, Daddy," she says, whispering softly. She bends her head lower and kisses my arm that's holding tight around her chest. "Thank you for everything. I promise to be your good girl. Always."

I mumble something back to her, but to be honest I

don't remember what it is. Don't hold it against me or anything. I'm tired, and Fiona's tired, and she's mumbling back to me, too. We have some kind of mumbled conversation that I'm pretty sure neither of us remembers.

It's nice, though. This is nice. Yes, I'm going to hell, but for now, everything is nice.

I fall asleep with Fiona in my arms and for a brief moment I wonder how I ever fell asleep without her.

FIONA

I sleep and I cuddle with Daddy and I dream about him all night long. In my dreams we're together now. We're a couple and we're dating and it's the best and most amazing thing in the entire world. He takes care of me and protects me from everything, and he loves me so much.

When I wake up from my dream, I'm smiling and holding onto Daddy. He's already awake and he smiles back at me. I don't know what time it is but it looks like it's starting to get bright out already. Not too much, and the sun is just barely peeking over the horizon, but it'll be all the way up really soon.

"Hi, Daddy," I say to him, blushing a little.

"Hey, baby," he says. "Did you sleep well?"

"I slept really well," I tell him, being extra honest. "I had some really good dreams, too. I wish they were real, but I know maybe they can't be, and that's alright, but I'm still really happy right now."

"Good," he says with a smile. "I'm glad."

Daddy leaves me for a second to reach for his phone on the bedside table. He looks at it quick and then puts it back. I just watch him, smiling the entire time.

"What time is it?" I ask him. "When do we have to get up?"

"Soon," he says with a little sadness in his voice. No, don't be sad, Daddy! "We have about twenty minutes before you should probably sneak back into Emily's room. It might be a good idea if you leave now."

"I don't want to leave," I tell him. "I want to cuddle with you."

"Oh yeah?" he asks, grinning at me. "That's it?"

"I don't know. Can we do anything else besides cuddling?" I ask him with a giggle.

"In twenty minutes? I think we could probably come up with something..."

I smile at him, trying to be all sweet and innocent. While I'm smiling, I reach between Daddy's legs to see just what exactly he might have in mind. Judging by what I find, I think we can definitely come up with something...

"What's this, Daddy?" I ask him, playing coy. "Is this just what happens when you wake up? I've heard it happens for a lot of guys."

"Sometimes," Daddy says, looking down and watching me stroke his cock slowly. "It's also what happens when I wake up next to my beautiful baby girl."

"Can I taste it, Daddy?" I ask him. "Can I try to see if I can get you off with my mouth?"

"Of course, Fiona," Daddy says to me, grinning. "Just

don't get frustrated if you can't, alright? Last night was incredible and I don't know if--"

Nope! I won't accept that! I'm going to do my best to please Daddy and that's that. I scurry lower down the bed and hop up a little and jump between his legs where his large, throbbing cock is waiting for me. Daddy laughs at my enthusiasm and pulls himself back a little, propping himself up so he's sitting and leaning back against the headboard. I scamper after him, following the bob of his cock.

I'm excited. I'm really really excited to see if I can do this for Daddy...

I take Daddy's cock in one of my hands and play with him slowly. I love the way he feels in my fingers, all throbbing and twitching. I go up and down slowly, watching Daddy's cock tremble in my grip. Daddy grins at me one last time before abandoning everything. He leans his head back and looks up at the ceiling and closes his eyes.

I open my mouth wide. I'm not entirely sure how to do this because I haven't done it before, but I want to make sure I can do it good. I want to make sure Daddy's cock fits in my mouth and that I don't use my teeth and I make him cum down my throat. I want to taste it and I want to see the look on his face when I make him feel so good that he can't help but cum a lot for me.

My lips touch against the head of Daddy's cock. He groans softly and then mutters some words of encouragement. I'm too caught up in doing what I'm doing to hear what he's saying, though.

Slow, careful, I wrap my lips around Daddy's cock and

then lower myself. A little bit, and then a little more. I squeeze his cock tight in my fingers, which I think he likes because he throbs really hard, and then I gently slide my lips down his shaft as far as I can go.

I can only take half of Daddy's cock in my mouth before the head touches against the back of my throat. I let it sit there for a second, enjoying the feeling of it. How do I take all of Daddy's cock in my mouth, though? I don't really know, but that's a question I'd like to answer sometime.

Later. Hopefully there'll be a later.

I slide back up Daddy's cock, trailing my tongue along the underside of his shaft. When I'm all the way at the top, I go back down. I stroke Daddy slowly like this, up with my mouth and hand, and then down, my lips and fingers sliding perfectly in sync.

Daddy grunts. Instinctive, without saying anything, he grabs my head. His fingers wrap around my hair, pulling tight but not too hard. The next time I go down, he holds me there for a second, then two seconds, three seconds, and...

My eyes start to water a little and I choke on Daddy's cock. Not too much, though. I swallow and gasp, which I realize sends a little more of Daddy's cock into my mouth. The head of his cock slides into my throat and I breathe through my nose so I can try to swallow a little more, but then Daddy pulls me back up by my hair.

"Fuck, baby," Daddy says with a groan. "I got excited there. Sorry. Are you alright?"

"I'm good, Daddy!" I say, cheery.

I say this, but a few tears slip down my cheeks. I'm not crying or anything, it just kind of happened when I started to choke a little. Daddy looks down at me and smiles. He reaches with his free hand and wipes away my tears. It's really sweet and nice, but then Daddy does something completely different with his hand...

He caresses my cheek lightly, tucking the tips of his fingers under my chin. His thumb sneaks out and traces softly against my lips. I kiss his thumb and then part my lips slightly. Daddy tickles my lower lip, on the outside first and then a little inside my mouth. He pushes his thumb slowly into my mouth until he's touching my tongue.

"Lick it, baby," he commands me.

I want to lick it so bad. I want to do anything and everything for Daddy.

I tease his thumb with my tongue, licking around the bottom and then up and around, pressing into the curves and lines by his nail. Daddy presses his thumb into my mouth even more until it's harder and harder for me to use my tongue. His fingers grab my cheek a little, holding me tight. I look up at him with my lips parted slightly as I suck on his thumb.

He smiles down at me. I don't know how to explain it, but no one's ever smiled at me like this before. It's a proud, happy smile, like I'm doing really good right now. I'm Daddy's good little girl and he's so happy with me. I melt and almost want to curl up into a ball in Daddy's lap and cuddle with him and giggle and snuggle forever.

I can't do that, though! I have things to do and they're *very* important.

Daddy pulls his thumb from my mouth and slowly moves his hand away. His cock bounces in front of me, eager for my lips. I don't want to keep Daddy waiting, so...

I go quick this time, taking as much of him as I can into my mouth. Daddy lets out a sharp hiss. His fingers are still in my hair from before. He grinds me against his cock roughly, pulling my hair. I know Daddy doesn't mean to hurt me, though. I surprised him and this is his reaction. It's pretty hot, to be honest. I'm excited, and I kind of want to stop and sit in Daddy's lap and take his cock inside me, in my tight little pussy, but I also want to make him cum with my mouth.

I swallow on my own this time now that I know what to expect. I choke a little, but I push past it, swallowing the head of Daddy's cock. He spasms and twitches under me, his entire body shaking. Daddy grunts and groans and grabs my hair.

"Fuck, fuck! Holy fucking... Fiona... I..."

Cum for me! Please, Daddy?

I think he's about to. I really really do. Does that mean I did a good job? I'm Daddy's good girl?

I don't get to find out. Someone knocks on Daddy's bedroom door. We both freeze for a second, confused in our lust. Daddy's eyes go wide and he lets go of my hair, slams his hand on his bedside table, and grabs his phone. Checking it with a frantic look in his eyes, he just sits there in a daze. After a couple seconds and another knock at his door, he turns the phone towards me.

I still have his cock in my mouth. I haven't swallowed since the first knock, though. Apparently when you have a cock in your mouth it's hard to stop yourself from drooling, too. Saliva drips from my lips, sliding down Daddy's shaft and pooling on his balls.

The timer on his phone shows that we should still have time. At least ten minutes to be exact. And...

Then comes the third knock. "Daddy? Grey? Are you awake? Can I come in? Have you seen Fiona? She's not in my room. I don't know where she is."

Yup... that's Emily.

GREY

You have no fucking idea how much I want to cum right now. I want to ignore my sister banging on my bedroom door, and I want to grab Fiona's head, shove her as far onto my cock as I can, and cum into that beautiful fucking throat of hers. I want to watch her as she smiles at me with her eyes even though a handful of tears are streaming down her cheeks. I want to see her throat bulge a little as she swallows every last drop of my cum, and then I want to pull her off of my cock and listen to her gasping for air.

I don't know why I want to do any of that. Maybe because I'm fucked up. What else do you want me to say?

I can't, though. Fiona's freaking out, and I'm freaking out, and I'm wondering if I locked my bedroom door. What if Emily comes in right now and catches us? Holy fucking shit, do you know how bad that'd be? I do. It'd be terrible. How the fuck would I explain this to her?

I mean, so yeah, Fiona's an adult. She can make her

own decisions. Technically there's nothing wrong with this. Try explaining that to my sister, though. Try telling her that it's perfectly fine for me to throatfuck her best friend. Let's not even get into the fact that my room probably smells heavily of sex from everything Fiona and I did last night.

Yeah... I'm screwed.

"Hold on!" I say to Emily.

Fiona stares at me, wide-eyed. "I'm sorry! I'm so sorry, Daddy! I shouldn't have... I..."

"Shh," I tell her. "It's fine. Just... just go hide in the bathroom. Turn on the shower. I'll handle this. I'll tell Emily that something was wrong with the shower upstairs so you asked me if you could use mine. The hot water or whatever. It wasn't working. Yeah."

"Daddy, what are you doing?" Emily asks, pounding on the door again. "Is Fiona in there?"

Fiona scrambles off my bed and scampers into the bathroom. I stare at her fine as fuck ass the entire time, just watching it bounce wildly as she runs away. Once she's in the bathroom, she closes the door quick. I jump out of bed, grab a random pair of pajama pants I find on the floor, toss them on, and go to let my sister in.

Before I open the door, I realize Fiona's pajamas are just scattered everywhere in my room. Fuck! I pick them up and toss them to the other side of my bed, hoping beyond hope that Emily doesn't see them if she tries to come inside.

I can explain some things, but I don't think I can explain that one. Why did Fiona strip down in your room before going into the shower, Daddy? You saw her naked? Well, that's a good question, Emily, and...

Yeah. Let's not even go there, alright?

I open the door shirtless. Emily tilts her head to the side and stares at me cockeyed for a second before craning her neck and peeking into the rest of my room.

"What?" I ask her. "Why are you being so loud?"

"What took you so long? I can't find Fiona," she says. "Have you seen her?"

"Yeah," I say. Act casual, Grey. You can do this. "Fiona woke up early and she wanted to take a shower so she wouldn't get in your way before we had to leave. The hot water wasn't working, though. She asked if she could use my shower instead."

"Um, the hot water wasn't working upstairs, but it's working down here?" she asks. "How is that even possible?"

Fuck. Uh...

I shrug, all nonchalant or something. "It might be something with the pipes," I say. "I'll get a plumber to come check them out later. No big deal."

"Fiona's in the shower now?" Emily asks, glancing at my closed bathroom door.

"Yeah? She should be out soon," I tell her.

"I'm going to go check the water upstairs," she says.

Well... double fuck. I didn't think this through very well. Obviously the hot water is fine.

I chase after Emily as she hurries back upstairs to her bathroom. She slides in and turns on the hot water quick. I just stand in the doorway, acting oblivious. After a few seconds, she holds her hand under the running water. I'm going to assume it's warm, because, you know, it should be. If not, I guess I really do have to call a plumber, and that kind of pisses me off.

"The water's fine," Emily says. "Huh. Weird! Maybe we just ran out for a second or something?"

"Yeah, actually, you know... I was doing laundry right before Fiona came down so maybe that had something to do with it."

"Daddy!" Emily scolds me. "You need to be careful. If you were running a load using hot water that could definitely make the water colder for a second, but you can't just wash everything on hot, you know? It's not good for your clothes. You need to check the washing instructions first."

"Oh," I say. Please, Emily, please please please don't go check the laundry. I shouldn't have even said that. "Yeah, uh... whoops?"

"It's *your* clothes," Emily says, hands on her hips. "If you want to ruin them, be my guest, but don't come complaining to me after."

She turns the bathtub faucet off and stands up, shaking her head at me. I just kind of take it, because I'm walking a fine line here and I'm pretty sure at any moment I might step over it and fuck everything up. And... yeah... let's not. I don't even want to try.

"I'm worried about Fiona," Emily says after a few seconds. "I'm worried about her being here all alone without me when I'm at college. I wish she was going to college with me, too."

"Yeah, I know," I tell her. "Don't get too wrapped up in it, though. You still need to go to college. It's for the best."

"Well yeah, duh," Emily says, giving me a dirty look. "I know that, Daddy. It's just... I mean, I'm excited about college, you know? But I'm worried about Fiona. And it's going to be hard without her. She's my best friend and I miss her already. That's why I woke up early. I thought we could all go out to breakfast together?"

"Sure," I say with a smile. "That sounds good."

"Can you make sure she's alright, Daddy?" Emily asks. "When I'm gone, I mean. Can you take care of her? And maybe you two can come visit me together on weekends or I'll come back here and hang out, and--"

"Emily, calm down," I say, shaking my head and laughing. "I think I can manage. It sounds like a good idea. I'll make sure Fiona's fine, alright?"

"Good!" Emily says, grinning at me. "Just don't have too much fun without me. She's my best friend, Daddy! Don't like... steal her away or anything."

"You're weird," I tell her, making a face. "Where would I even steal her away to?"

"Um, you're bedroom?" Emily says.

Wait, uh... *what?* Fuck. She fucking knows! How'd she figure it out? I try not to panic. I can come up with an excuse. What excuse? I don't know. I bet it was the sex smell. My bedroom probably reeks of sex, because a lot of sex happened last night. Just being honest there. It really did.

"What's that look on your face for?" Emily asks, suspicious. "Don't deny it. She's in your bathroom right now. You told me so!"

"Oh," I say. "Yeah, uh... right. Well, you don't have to worry about me stealing her away to my bedroom again. The hot water is fine, so we're all good."

"Fiona forgot her clothes, by the way," Emily says, shaking her head. "I swear, I don't know what she's going to do without me around. She's kind of forgetful, Daddy. I'll go get them and bring them to her, alright? Don't worry."

Emily heads to her room to grab Fiona's clothes. Not the pajamas, which are currently laying on my bedroom floor. They're... they're laying on my... yeah... not in the bathroom, where they should be.

Fuck.

I leap down the stairs while Emily's still in her room getting Fiona's clothes. Sprinting down the hall to my bedroom, I launch myself inside, grab every last thing that even remotely looks like it could belong to Fiona, wrench open the bathroom door, and...

Standing there, slick and wet, completely naked, is Fiona. I stare at her hard. My cock twitches in my pants and I suddenly remember that I didn't have a chance to get off just a few minutes ago. I was so fucking close, but...

Do you know how tempting this is? How much I want to just grab Fiona, shove her onto my bed, and thrust my cock deep inside her. I don't even think it'd take much more than that. One thrust, just in, and I'm pretty sure I'd be filling her the fuck up with everything I've got.

I can't do that. I really want to do that, but I can't. Emily's going to be here any moment, so...

I thrust Fiona's clothes at her, give her a discerning look, and then slam the bathroom door in her face. Look, I didn't mean to slam it in her face. In hindsight, maybe that was kind of a dick move. It just sort of happened.

Once I'm done I, uh... I just pretend I'm making the bed. Except I really need to wash my sheets. They're dry now, but they're kind of ripe after being completely soaked by me and Fiona last night. I'm sorry. Actually, I'm not. Not even sorry. Sorry for not being sorry.

Emily comes waltzing into my room with Fiona's clothes. She gives me a weird look.

"What?" I ask her.

"Why are you standing right by the bathroom door?" she asks.

"What? I'm not. I'm making my bed."

"I guess!"

"Shut up. Go give Fiona her clothes."

"Go outside," Emily says, shaking a fist at me. "What if Fiona's naked?"

I don't answer, because I really don't think my sister wants to know what I think about Fiona being naked. Instead, I just give up. I walk out of my own bedroom, which is being completely taken over right now. My sister seriously has no sense of privacy. I get it, and maybe I haven't exactly been the strictest with her about it over the years, but I think I deserve my own bedroom and a little privacy now and then.

I probably don't deserve privacy when Fiona's involved. Who knows what'll happen? Don't tell Emily.

I head to the kitchen to get myself a glass of orange juice. I could probably use some vodka with it, but now's not the time.

FIONA

The rest of the morning goes fine. I shower up and Emily brings me my clothes. I wish Daddy were here, but he's off hiding somewhere. I feel bad that I didn't get to finish giving him a blowjob earlier, though. Maybe I can soon?

Emily's taking a shower now, so...

Cute and all dolled up with some of Emily's makeup, I search through the house for Daddy. I find him in his office. I don't like that. I know Daddy has to do work, but his office is right by the bathroom upstairs, which is where Emily is, and that kind of makes it hard to finish what I started earlier.

Daddy works away on his computer up here, typing some things. When he sees me standing in the doorway, he pauses and smiles at me.

"Hey," he says.

"Hi, Daddy," I say. "I'm sorry about earlier."

"No, it's... it's fine, Fiona," he says slowly.

"Was I a good girl, though?" I ask.

"Baby... that was amazing. You were a *very* good girl. It's just... uh... we can't do that right now."

"Later?" I ask him with a wink.

He doesn't say anything, but when I look towards his crotch I see a nice outline of his hard cock trapped in his pants.

"Daddy?" I ask him. "Emily said that you promised to take care of me and make sure I'm alright when she's away at college. Is that true?"

Daddy swallows hard and looks me up and down. I let him ogle me for a second, posing for him. I arch my back and push my breasts out, then I turn sideways and pop my ass out for him while I run my hands up and down the door casing of his office, sensual and sleek.

"You're being naughty right now, Fiona," Daddy says with a hint of a growl.

"Oops!" I say, playful. "Does that mean you need to spank me?"

"Get your naughty ass over here," he says.

I hurry to Daddy's side. He wraps his arm around my waist and pulls me into his lap. I nuzzle against his neck and hold him tight, hugging him close.

"I did tell Emily I'd keep an eye on you," he says.

"Will you really?" I ask.

"I'll try," he says, honest. "I don't think I'm good for you, Fiona. I still think you should find someone your own age, and I think you should enjoy life and experience things while you still can."

"Does that mean you aren't going to spank me later?" I ask him, quirking my head to the side and pouting.

"No, your ass is mine," he says with a smirk. "Not now. Probably not even today. Once I get back from bringing Emily to college, though... yeah... I expect you to be here as soon as I call you. You can't be naughty and expect to get away with it, Fiona. After I spank your ass and you promise to be good, we can talk about the rest."

The rest...

Does that mean what I think it means? I don't know. I'm excited, though. I want to be with Daddy so bad. I got a taste last night and then more this morning and now I can't stop thinking about it.

"Go," he says, pushing me gently off his lap. "Emily will be out soon and then we'll head to breakfast."

I hop up off his lap and start to scurry away. Daddy grabs my waist before I can leave, then he swats my butt quick. It's not the same as his regular spankings, but it still makes me yelp. I giggle and squirm in his arms and he pulls me back.

"You're going to leave without giving me a kiss?" he asks, grinning at me.

"Whoops. Sorry, Daddy!" I say.

I wrap my arms around his neck and kiss him on the lips. It's soft and sweet at first, but then Daddy kisses me back harder. Our tongues start to dance and play with each other and before I know it we're making out.

The bathroom door in the hallway outside Daddy's office opens up. Emily shouts from the doorway, "Fiona! Can you help me with my makeup? Please!"

Um...

Daddy lets me go. I hop off his lap and skip to the bathroom quick. Emily's just standing there, looking towards her room. She's dressed and all, so it's not like anything weird is happening.

Except, you know, me coming from the direction of Daddy's office.

Um...

"Were you in Daddy's office?" Emily asks me. "Is he in there?"

"Oh, yup," I say. "I was just saying hi. He's working."

"You can't bother him when he's working, Fiona," Emily says, exasperated, shaking her head at me.

"I know, I know," I say. Turning back the way I came, I shout out, "Sorry, Daddy! I didn't mean to interrupt you!"

Daddy grunts and shakes his head at me.

"See? He gets grumpy," Emily says.

It's true, but I bet I could make Daddy happy.

Later, right? That's what he said.

The rest...

I can't wait! I know I can make Daddy happy.

A NOTE FROM MIA

Make sure you don't miss any of my new releases by
signing up for my VIP readers list!
Cherrylily.com/Mia

You can also find me on Facebook for more sneak peeks
and updates here:
Facebook.com/MiaClarkWrites

First things first!

I've included a few of the chapters from my Stepbrother With Benefits series after this, so if you haven't
read that yet, make sure to check those out.

Now that that's out of the way, let's get into the regular
notes!

If you've never read one of my books before, I like to
include notes at the end to tell you a little about the story

characters so we can kind of talk about them
r. This story is a little different from Stepbrother
Benefits, so I kind of wanted to tell you about some
of the inspiration behind it.

I saw some "Daddy Romance" books on Amazon and
at first I was like, um... I do not know...

And then I realized one of my favorite things in BDSM
is something called DD/lg or Daddy Dom / little girl.
Now, this isn't really your Fifty Shades type of BDSM.
Also, it can mean a lot of things, as um... well, BDSM can
be a lot of things, haha. What I like about DD/lg is that to
me it's more playful and cute.

I don't think of it as very hardcore, and I think of it as
more of an unconditional loving relationship where the
submissive aims to please, and the dom is trying to guide
her to become a better person with rules and stuff. The
rules don't have to be crazy or anything, but in Grey and
Fiona's case it might include not stroking his cock with her
foot while they're eating dinner in a restaurant.

But that's just me! Everyone has different ideas about it.
I thought about adding my own take on it as a post on the
Cherrylily site I share with some other authors, but I'm not
sure. Would you be interested in that? Email me or
message me on Facebook and I'll see what I can do! Maybe
I'll even make it the secret link at the back of this book for
a little while. Hmm...

That's where the spanking in this book came from,
though. Maybe Grey can have fun with Fiona in different
ways in the future, but for now I just wanted it to be fun,
playful, and easy. Nothing crazy, just good sexy times

between the two of them with a little taboo forbidden romance added in there since they can't really tell Emily about this.

Or can they? I don't know...

Speaking of that, I know I left the ending a little open. I don't want to say it's a cliffhanger, because I think it can end there. I'm fine with that, and if you like the story as it is then there we go! It'll be over, and we can imagine it however we want. I don't know if Emily will be all that mad about Fiona being with Grey, and I'm sure it'll be easier for Fiona since she doesn't have a place to stay anymore since her mom kind of kicked her out, so...

Do you want more, though? I'm definitely open to writing more books like this and continuing the story, but I don't want you to think that it's necessary or anything. If you want more, definitely let me know! Email me, message me on Facebook, or leave a review on Amazon and I will happily consider Grey and Fiona's future together, probably with some more spanking, and definitely with more sexy yoga scenes!

Or we can leave it like it is! That one is up to you, but I hope you enjoyed the story either way.

If you loved Grey and Fiona, I'd love it if you left me a review and let me know what you think! I enjoy reading them and hearing your thoughts, and it helps me figure out what to write more of in the future. Did you like Grey and Fiona sneaking around, or do you think they should just come clean to Emily? Except... what will Emily think? Oh no.

Do you think Grey's right and Fiona should date other

people since she doesn't have experience, or maybe he should help her get more experience on his own? Also, I really liked the yoga part.

Maybe it would be fun to see Fiona get jealous if they go do yoga together while Emily's gone, and then Grey ends up dragging her back home and showing her that she's got nothing to worry about since she's all his and he doesn't plan on either of them sharing each other with anyone else?

Decisions, decisions...

I just hope you loved the story and that you're excited about Grey and Fiona. Definitely let me know what you think.

Thanks again for reading. I really appreciate it!

Bye for now!

~Mia

STEPBROTHER WITH BENEFITS 1
(TEASER)

Please enjoy this teaser from my bestselling Stepbrother With Benefits series!

∽

> *"Friends with benefits, stepbrother with benefits,*
>   *what's the difference?"*
> *"Um, we're not even friends, Ethan?"*

Rule #1 – *It's only supposed to last for a week...*

INTRODUCTION

How did I wind up naked, face down ass up on my bed, with my stepbrother behind me, thrusting hard into me, my face buried in a pillow to muffle my moans while our parents are downstairs making dinner and waiting for us to join them so we can eat? Well, that's a long story. To be honest, I'm not even sure how this started. It's so wrong, and I know we shouldn't be doing this, but then why does it feel so good? Why do I love it? Why am I...

I think I love it a little too much. I'm even starting to worry myself.

He leans over me and pins me to the bed, burying himself deep inside of me with one last thrust. I know what's coming next, but I can barely think anymore. My body's already betrayed me and given in to the delicious feeling of his thick, hard cock inside me. I've never had orgasms as powerful as the ones I have with Ethan, and this current climax is one of my stronger ones. My pussy milks his cock, my inner walls clenching against him as he cums inside of me.

I feel it, and it feels so perfect, so warm and soft despite the fact that he was just fucking me hard. I don't understand anything about Ethan. I don't know how he can be like this. He's some kind of walking contradiction. I don't know why we're in bed together.

I don't want to ever leave, though.

He stays inside of me, jet after jet of his cum filling me to the brim. I can feel it seeping out of me, just a little. It's going to leave a mess on my bed. I don't know how I'm supposed to explain this.

I just want to lay here, just a little longer, I want to stay here with him inside of me. I want to...

I want to lay back and cuddle with him and...

No. That's not part of our arrangement. We can't do that. My God, he's my brother! Stepbrother, I remind myself. But still.

He pulls out of me and slaps me on the ass.

"Let's go, Princess. Mom and Dad are waiting," Ethan says, cocky and confident as ever.

"I can't believe we did that," I say in disbelief. I laugh, but he just smirks at me.

"You know you loved it," he says, reaching for his pants on the floor.

There's something about the way he says it, something about how casual it sounds, but I feel like there's more to his words, too. I don't know why I feel like that, because this is Ethan we're talking about. He's a bad boy, and everyone knows it. No one and nothing can tame him. He does what he wants, when he wants. I didn't just love it, I love...

Stop, Ashley. Don't do this to yourself.

I thought I'd learned to deal with it. I mean, our parents have been married for three years already, so I should have figured him out by now, right? Nope, not really.

I lay on the bed and watch him put his pants on. They're loose around his waist and hang from his hips, even after he's zipped and buttoned them up. Ethan plays football in college--he even has a scholarship, though it's not like he needs it since his dad is rich--and he's got muscles in all the right places. That slick, perfect V angling from his hips to his crotch.

It's like an arrow pointing to everything I want. Or a warning sign telling me to run away because this is dangerous. Maybe Ethan's bad boy personality is rubbing off on me. I've been feeling really naughty lately, so I wouldn't be surprised.

I'm still naked from the waist down when he finishes putting his clothes back on. He stares at me, giving me a weird, confusing kind of look. Ethan walks back to the bed, leans over me, and without saying anything or even asking, he thrusts two fingers deep into my sex.

I gasp and my back arches before I can think or do or say anything. Somehow I manage to breathe out his name. "Ethan!"

"Listen, Ashley, you think you can get away with looking at me like that, laying on your bed with no pants on? Nah, I don't think so. You're still mine right now. Yeah, that's a good girl. Fuck, you're so sensitive. How many orgasms did you have? Tell me."

I whimper and beg him with little muttered words, but he ignores me.

"Tell me. Now. How many?"

"Four," I say, a whisper.

"Louder," Ethan says.

"Mom and Dad will... they'll hear us, Ethan. You need to stop."

"You think I care?"

It sounds harsh, but there's a subtle softness in his eyes. Ethan wouldn't hurt me, he wouldn't be mean to me. I don't expect you to understand, but it's a part of this, it's one of the rules we made together. The rules that we don't seem to be following anymore, since we were supposed to stop this when our parents came back...

"Tell me how many orgasms you had?" he asks me again. "Your pussy is mine, and I want you to keep track."

"Four," I say again, louder, but now it's a lie. "Five," I say, correcting myself, blushing.

My body spasms on the bed as my brother fingerfucks me, pushing past the grip of my orgasm, making me whimper and writhe in ecstatic release.

When he's done, when I'm finished, he pulls his fingers out of me and shoves them in my mouth. "Taste," he says.

I open my mouth without thinking and lick around his fingers, sucking them like they're his cock. I open my eyes and peek towards his crotch and notice that, yes, he's erect again. I really could be sucking his cock. Maybe I will. Maybe...

"Now put some damn pants on," he says, smiling, teasing me. "Mom and Dad are waiting for us."

ASHLEY

(Four Days Earlier)

"This isn't going to work."

"Huh?" I ask.

"Ashley, this isn't going to work. Have you thought about how we're going to do this? We're leaving for summer break. Right now. You're going back to your parents and I'm going back to mine. How are we going to do this?"

"Jake, I don't know what you're talking about."

And, I don't. I really don't, especially considering we just had sex. Literally. We're in Jake's dorm room while his roommate is out, and one thing led to another, and, well...

I don't usually do this. I don't want Jake to think I'm a... a slut or anything. We've only had sex once before, but I thought that since we were going back home for summer break, this was a good time to do it again. I won't be able to see him for a few months.

"Ash, you live five hours away from me. We'll be apart the whole summer. What kind of relationship is that?"

"Um... a long distance one?" I say.

He laughs, but it's not a nice laugh. Kind of a douchebag asshole laugh, actually. Which is really mean considering he just had his dick inside me. The least he could do is be a little nicer.

I can't believe I'm even thinking this. Nicer? Yeah, Ashley, um... he's your boyfriend! He *should* be nice to you. Duh?

"I don't do long distance relationships, babe," Jake says. "It's not my thing."

"So you're breaking up with me?" I ask, as if I couldn't say anything stupider at the moment.

Yes, I've got perfect grades, I was the top of my class in high school, and I've got three scholarships that will more than cover most of my first two years of college, but apparently I'm still dumb enough to have to ask if my boyfriend is breaking up with me.

"I'm not breaking up with you," he says.

"Oh," I say. He makes no sense to me.

"I'm just saying we can't do this. I can't go the entire summer without sex, babe. It's impossible."

"Oh." I have no idea where he's going with this.

"We'll take a break. See other people. At least for the summer. When we get back to school next year we can pick up where we left off."

"Wait..."

Look, I know what you're thinking. I'm not an idiot, alright? I'm really not. I just... I like Jake. I think. I'm not sure how I feel about him. I'd never had a boyfriend before college, and even then my boyfriends up until now haven't exactly been... boyfriends? I dated a couple of guys for a week or two, but that's it. Jake and I have been going out for a couple months now and I thought everything was going well, but...

Nope, apparently not.

"It's not you, it's me," he says.

"Yeah, obviously," I say. I know it's not me. What a stupid thing to say. He's the one breaking up with me!

Jake laughs. "It'll be fine. Go home and have a few one night stands or something. Learn how to be better in bed. You're kind of stiff, you know? You need to get a little more into it. When we come back to school next year, we can date again. Trial run or something? See how it goes. I've been putting up with you for now, but I really need someone who knows what they're doing, Ash. The sex just hasn't been that good. Sorry to put it out there like that."

"No," I say. "It's fine."

That's not what I want to say. I want to say more. I want to say something witty and funny and sarcastic. Because I don't think it's me. He's not very good in bed, either. Selfish and fast is about how I'd explain it, but I thought he liked me, so...

My God, I'm an idiot, aren't I?

I put my clothes on and rush to the door just as his roommate is coming back. His roommate accidentally blocks me from making a hasty retreat until we shuffle around to either side and I can get past him. I want to go. I want to run back to my room and pack and leave right now, because... because...

Jake is an asshole! I almost think about screaming it, but I stop myself. I can't do that. I'm the good girl, the girl with perfect grades, the girl everyone expects to go far in life. I'm...

I'm a doormat, apparently. I'm the girl whose boyfriend breaks up with her so he can sleep with other women during a two month summer break from college. Wow.

Really, wow.

"Text me sometime or something," Jake yells to me as I rush down the hall.

"Fuck you," I say. I want to shout it, but I don't. I whisper it to myself under my breath.

I'm Ashley Banks and I'm a good girl. Good girls don't swear and shout down the halls. I can't do that, even if I want to.

3

ETHAN

The school year's over. I'm supposed to be packing up to leave. Supposed to be, but yeah, guess what I'm doing instead? Something stupid.

A couple of guys from the team dragged me out to play shirts versus skins football on the field because the cheerleaders were doing some last hoorah celebration, complete with those fuckably short skirts they love to wear. Fuck. Those legs. That ass. Fuck. Just fuck.

I can't deal with this shit, man. You don't even know how fucking hard this is right now.

Shirts versus skins, but it devolved into skins versus skins soon enough. Who even gives a fuck what team we're on? No one, apparently. It's all some ruse to impress the cheerleaders, so it's not like it matters. And, yeah, it's working. They're doing their little cheer celebration, but they keep looking over at us. Can't say I blame them.

This is college football and we're in the prime of our

lives. Look, I'm kind of an asshole, alright? I know it. Everyone knows it. No reason to hide it.

I look good, though. Especially with a shirt off. Especially when I'm sweating, muscles tight, running around a field, throwing a football.

What position? Quarterback. Shouldn't it be obvious? I was born to be in the spotlight.

Probably helps that my dad's rich. Can't hurt at least.

The cheerleaders are done, and now they're just sitting on the bleachers watching us. Some of the guys pretend to have a huddle or some stupid shit, but it's all of them together. No offense, but what the fuck kind of huddle is that? Two teams would never huddle together. Doesn't make any goddamn sense.

"Last play, guys," someone says. "Make it good. Flashy. Then let's go get our water bottles. Make that flashy, too."

I almost laugh. *These guys*. They really need to get laid. I guess they're about to, so it's all good.

I do some flashy shit, throw the ball higher in the air than necessary so it looks cooler when someone catches it. I don't even care who, just someone. It works. They do. Is that guy supposed to be on my team? I can't tell anymore.

Stupid. This isn't real football, it's just stupid.

We're done. It's over. Walking. Yup.

You might be asking how someone drinks water from a water bottle in a flashy way. And if you're asking that, you need to stop and calm down a little because it's about to happen, so just sit there and see for yourself.

We all go get our water. I drink mine, because I'm thirsty, and not the kind of *thirsty* that these guys are.

Yeah, the cheerleaders are cute, but I don't need or want any of that pussy right now. They don't do much for me. I'm a bad boy, but I've still got standards, you know?

The rest of the guys get real into it, though. Drinking, but losing half the water, letting it splash down their faces, dripping past their throats, onto their bare chests. Dude, you're already sweaty from football, so I don't know what this is going to do.

Whatever. It works. Fucking A, it works. It's like cheerleader bait or some shit. They flock to the muscled meat in front of them. Solo, in pairs, or sometimes three at a time, each heading towards the man of their dreams.

Dreams. Ha! Yeah, right. You know how long dreams last? One night. Then you forget about them when you wake up in the morning. This is pretty much the same thing, but it'll be even shorter. We're all leaving this afternoon and going back home.

Home.

A bunch of cheerleaders flock towards me, even though I didn't put on a show for them. Five. More than the other guys. I briefly wonder if I could have them all at the same time. Greedy, much? What the fuck would I even do with five girls at once? I don't know, but I wouldn't mind finding out sometime. I've got two hands, a cock, and a mouth. I'm sure the last girl can think of something to do, too. It'll work.

"Hey, Ethan."

"Hey, Chelsea," I say.

"Hey, Ethan."

This goes on. And on. Five times. Fuck my life.

Chelsea, Jaime, Robin, Maxi, and Bella. I'm not that much of a dick, alright? I do know what their names are. I've talked to them before. I'm on the football team and they're cheerleaders. Get off my case.

Yes, fuck you, I slept with Bella. That's it. Just her. Alright, look, shut the fuck up, I made out with Chelsea and Robin at the same time, and maybe I fingered Jaime, and, yes, I let Maxi suck my cock, but that's it.

Don't fucking judge me.

"Look, this is real interesting," I say, even though they've been babbling on for five minutes and I don't remember a word of what they said. "I've got to go, though. Plane to catch."

"Awww."

"Awww."

Five of those. Fuck my life. Seriously, just fuck it.

"I'll see you next year, though. Good job uh... cheering?"

They actually do a good job, so it's not like this is a stretch, but it sounds goofy as fuck. They act like it's the nicest compliment anyone's ever given them, though.

"Thanks, Ethan!"

You know the drill. Five of those. Wow, seriously?

"Talk to you ladies later," I say.

I think that's it. Or I thought that was it, but when I start to walk away, I've got a following. Yeah, you guessed it, five.

"Do you need help packing?" Chelsea asks.

"Back in your room?" Maxi adds.

"We don't mind." That's Robin.

"If we help you pack fast..." Jaime.

Bella's not even subtle. She mimes sucking my cock by poking her tongue in her cheek and moving her hand in front of her mouth when she thinks no one else is looking. The other girls giggle when they see her.

I don't even fucking know what is going on anymore. Is this real life? Fuck.

"I'm done packing," I lie. "Have to leave now, actually. Seriously, my plane's leaving in an hour. I'm going to be late." Another lie, I've got four hours and the plane isn't going to leave without me.

Did I mention my dad's rich? Private company jet. You have no idea how good that shit is. Seriously, it's good.

They all make a sad little pouty face, but I just laugh and keep on walking. I notice some of the other guys nearby staring at me like I'm insane.

Hey, fuck you, I'm not insane. I'm Ethan Colton, cocky asshole, arrogant prick, and bad boy extraordinaire. I could fuck every girl here if I wanted to, but it's getting kind of old. I need a change of pace.

ABOUT THE AUTHOR

Mia likes to have fun in all aspects of her life. Whether she's out enjoying the beautiful weather or spending time at home reading a book, a smile is never far from her face. She's prone to randomly laughing at nothing in particular except for whatever idea amuses her at any given moment.

Sometimes you just need to enjoy life, right?

She loves to read, dance, and explore outdoors. Chamomile tea and bubble baths are two of her favorite things. Flowers are especially nice, and she could get lost in a garden if it's big enough and no one's around to remind her that there are other things to do.

She lives in New Hampshire, where the weather is beautiful and the autumn colors are amazing.

You can find the rest of her books at:

www.amazon.com/author/mia-clark

You can also email her any time at Mia@Cherrylily.com if you have questions, comments, or if you'd just like to say hi!

Made in the USA
San Bernardino, CA
23 June 2019